Arlo and Jake Deep Cover

Book Four of the Adventures of Arlo and Jake

By

Gary Alan Henson

A Magnus Somnium Publication

Lewisville, Texas

Copyright © 2018 by Gary Alan Henson

Revision 1 September 2018

All rights reserved. No part of this publication may be reproduced electronically, mechanically, by photocopy, recording, or any other method except for brief quotations in reviews, without the prior permission of the copyright owner.

This is a work of fiction. References to names, characters, places and incidents either are the product of the author's imagination or are used fictitiously, and any resemblance to any actual persons, living or dead, events or locales is entirely coincidental.

Plant you butt in your favorite patio chair, sit back with a hot plate of nachos and a cold Fat Tire.

Enjoy the ride!

Acknowledgments

Once more into the Great Void we go! The support of my wife, Debbie, and my friends across the Twitter Verse make this book possible.

Arlo says 'Thank you!'

Books by Gary Alan Henson

Science Fiction

'Arlo and Jake Enlist' (2013)

'Arlo and Jake Galactic Boot Camp' (2014)

'Arlo and Jake Lost Partner' (2015)

'Arlo and Jake Deep Cover (2018)

Ghost Stories and Paranormal

'Genome' (2006)

'Etchings' (2015)

'Walk with Me' (2016)

Chapter One

"Convoy Romero, this is Strantos Prime. All vessels report pre-transit status."

Commander John Sprague stands beside his Captain's chair, straightening his immaculate tunic. He surveys the ordered chaos on the bridge of the 'Strantos'. His heart swells with pride watching the efficiency and intensity of his officers and crew as they perform the myriad of tasks that keep his ship functioning, minute to minute. Unconsciously, he shifts his left arm, fist clinched tightly, into his back, planting it firmly into his kidney. His posture exudes confidence and control.

Five bridge stations form a half circle in front of him with his chair at the center. Operations, Weapons, Communications, Engineering and Navigation each have a senior enlisted crewman or an officer at the station, scanning their consoles and screens, communicating with voice, brain implants and hand signals. The SBO, the Senior Bridge Officer, is standing just below the Captain, keeping an eye on each station, ready to correct or assist if necessary.

The senior enlisted Engineering crewman, Senior Chief Wakkon, also known as the 'Bull Nuke', stands at attention just to the left of the Captain's chair. Wakkon is a stout Gruenite, his short cropped hair an unusual grey due to his recent refusal to undergo rejuvenation. Each serviceman has the option to rejuv periodically or not. The Senior Chief's long service to the FTG is ending. He's seen far too much death and destruction in the last four hundred years. He's ready to live out his remaining life on his home world, letting the Universe continue without him.

He snaps a sharp salute to the Captain and says, "Engineering is fully operational, sir. You have full power and transit capability."

The Captain returns the salute to acknowledge the report. "Well done Bull. Give my complements to the watch," He turns again to the bridge stations, his focus on the mission once more. The Bull spins on his heels and breaks into a lope towards his domain in the bowels of the ship.

FTG Strantos is a light Cruiser in the service of the Federation of Thirteen Galaxies. She's a veteran ship, with a battle-tested crew. The ship and crew have distinguished themselves repeatedly against the forces of the GHA, the Galactic Houses of Aquinoxous. The GHA is a federation of dozens of aquatic species whose home worlds are mostly water.

The FTG Fleet is in an ongoing war to prevent the GHA from aquaforming and colonizing the galaxies, destroying whatever life forms exists as they advance. The GHA forces spread like a plague across the Galaxies swallowing up world after world. Lately the conflict is not going well for the FTG. Early attempts to coexist in peace failed repeatedly. The GHA consider non-aquatic species to be inferior and a pestilence on the Universe. They consider it a duty to eradicate all terra firma based species.

Most ships like the Strantos are on rotating operations, doing double and triple duty when not in space dock. Before returning to the front line after a repair and refit, they draw several support missions, protecting convoys of desperately needed equipment and supplies to outlying systems hit hard by the fighting. The GHA's new tactic of somehow finding and hitting these convoys and then running has been stretching the FTG's resources to the limit.

This should be a routine resupply mission, but Sprague knows every mission is dangerous these days. On the aft bridge screens, he watches his convoy of civilian supply ships maneuvering into a pre-transit formation, behind the Strantos. Three large cargo ships, six medium tankers loaded with liquids and foodstuffs, and twelve repair, medical and construction vessels. The Planetary System FFooFF desperately needs this cargo. The FTG barely managed to stop GHA forces from overrunning two of its planets, but not before their inhabitants suffered major surface damage and loss of life.

Sprague says, "John Boy! Any intel that would delay our mission at this point?"

'John Boy' is his alias for the ship's Artificial Intelligence. The AI is constantly monitoring the Strantos' condition, the Fleet communications and a thousand other matters. Without the AI it would be impossible to manage the myriad tasks that allow a ship to function, much less transit through space.

Since the Captain asked the question aloud, Ship responds over the bridge's comm system. "No sir. All Fleet communication is a 'Go' to proceed."

Time to get this mission underway. He turns sharply to his Executive Officer, eyebrows raised slightly. "How are our charges behaving, XO? If it's convenient, I would like to transit before the supplies rot in their holds."

Lieutenant Eva Bonnet J'Kal, a tall, lithe Talusha, smooths the short, white fur under her pointed chin and smiles, baring the small pointed teeth of her species. The Talusha are humanoids with notable feline features. A soft, fine fur covers her body. She has deep green eyes with long lashes, high cheek bones and long, sharp, retractable talons. They are fierce warriors, quick and agile. They excel in leadership positions like Executive and Commanding Officers, preferring to lead rather than to follow.

The XO is leaning over the Communications Console conferring with the operator, her crimson fingernails extended and tapping impatiently on the poor crewman's shoulder. To his credit, CT3 Hoekstra, a Spritezoid with bright red, spikey hair on his head, does not flinch, his focus centered on the competing voices from around the bridge and from his brain implant.

J'Kal straightens up from the console, listening to the same communications through her own implant. "They are surprisingly efficient for a civilian convoy, sir. Ten ships are primed and ready to fold. Nine will be ready shortly. Only one straggler this time, sir. A late addition to the convoy. The 'Crak Toh' reports they had an engine core restart. They request a five minute delay in transit to allow them time to bring their engines online and join the convoy."

Irritated at the delay, Sprague's jaw tightens. "I'm of a mind to leave them XO, I want to keep to our schedule." He rubs his chin, debating what to do. "What is her cargo?"

J'Kal taps a code on her arm comtat. The 'command tattoo' flares into life, tracing thin bright burnt-gold lines through the bionic circuitry embedded into her skin. Swirls of color race around the tattoo, mixing with other colors of her multiple other comtats as they respond to her request. Her arm seems alive with pulsing lines of multicolored light. In seconds, the information is relayed to the implant in her cranium.

"I've scanned her manifest, sir. She's carrying power modules, medicines and AI matrix-material. All critically needed at our destination," she says disappointingly. "Sorry, sir, I believe we'll need to wait for them."

"Damn!" Sprague was also hoping the cargo was inconsequential to the mission. He hated the sloppy nature of civilian ships.

"Very well. We leave in three, XO. See to it, if you please. And send Command the details of that ship, I don't want it to delay future missions." Sprague shifts his focus to the forward screens, his thoughts turning to the transit ahead, the convoy mission and a thousand other things a ship's commander must think about, moment by moment. He knows that J'Kal will have everything ready in two minutes, just to impress him.

The Captain of the Strantos, a tall rugged human, instinctively lets his mind separate, one part surveying the bridge activities, listening to each command station's communication, checking the engine room's status via his implant and a dozen other details. The other part savors this moment, relishing the intense anticipation of a new mission and a new adventure. This may be a simple supply convoy, but each mission has its own challenges and Sprague lives for those challenges. They give meaning to his life.

His career in the FTG has been much like others who give their lives in service to others. Moments of chaos and gut wrenching terror interspersed with long periods of mind numbing routine. He feels his excitement rising and struggles to maintain the cool, professional exterior demanded of his position. A transit begins another adventure, another chance to explore and meet whatever challenges the Universe throws at his ship.

J'Kal's mind is a whirlwind of activity, pulling her in a dozen directions at the same time. Her eyes are wide and bright, taking in everything on the bridge as if in slow motion. Nothing escapes her notice. Each crewman is performing up to her demanding standards, without any prodding from her. The Strantos has been an exhilarating billet, easily the best crew she has had the pleasure to serve with.

WEPS, the Weapons Officer, is going over his status for the third time, making sure his department has everything online and 'green lit' meaning ready for action.

A-Gang is making the last minute adjustments to a gravity field generator that's acting up. The Auxiliary Division is constantly roaming the ship, making repairs and installing refit improvements from FTG Command. The A-Gang robots can handle everything from tweaking communications equipment to the installation and repair of the monstrous weapons clusters on the outer hull. But the men and women of that crew are always there, making decisions, monitoring and adjusting the work.

Chief Engineer Cheng reports that main engines are ready to fold space for the transit. All engineering stations reporting systems are green to go.

She checks off each department as she goes through her mental list. Her last checkpoint is the Strantos' AI, who confirms all is ready for the transit.

Sprague queries his comtat for the time and convoy status and smiles slightly. Any moment now, J'Kal will be…

"Strantos and all convoy ships report ready for transit, sir." Her face shares her commander's delight in starting another mission. "Permission to commence, sir."

"Well done, XO. Permission granted."

The XO turns towards the forward screens. She taps the Communications operator on the shoulder and says, "Key me into the convoy frequency, Comm."

Congratulating himself on his self-control for not flinching again, the Communications Officer makes the correct connections. "Ready, sir."

J'Kal's voice is crisp and precise. "All vessels, Convoy Romero. Prepare to transit. Fold in five, four, three, two, one…"

Space warps around the small ill-fated group of ships.

Chapter Two

"I don't understand, Arlo, what happened between you and Tia? You were closer than two ticks on a dog's butt. I thought you guys were solid."

I take another bite of my brat and kraut sandwich, licking the spicy mustard from my lips. Hot juicy goodness fills my senses. The taste, smell, even the sound of the crisp brat skin crunching in my mouth is amazing. I set the bun down to wipe my mouth with a napkin and raise the cold mug of simulated Fat Tire beer. A quick gulp of the burning cold brew washes the tasty mouthful down.

Crew's lounge Twenty-Two forward, is packed for the afternoon shift lunch hour. Robo- waiters are buzzing around with food and drinks jostling precariously on trays held high. The soft murmur of hundreds of galactic species in pursuit of food and company fills the large room. Crewmen are huddled around tables of all sizes, downing a dizzying assortment of grub, some of it desperately trying to escape being eaten.

As usual, the wall screens around the room are projecting a scene from some crewman's home word. At the moment, we're surrounded by a hellish nightmare of lava spewing red-black volcanoes, dense dirty yellow clouds of gas whipping huge gray-green dust devils into a frenzy. Everywhere I look there are enormous jagged columns of lightning and flashes of gray light exploding inside the vapors. I glance around at the chaotic scene, my spine tingling from the thought of being on that planet. *There's one vacation spot that is not on my bucket list!*

Relishing the tastes and smells and sounds around me, I set the mug back on the table and lean back in the chair. I gaze into the freaky cadmium-yellow eyes of my partner, Arlo. My little friend's table perch puts him high enough to make conversation seem normal, even if it is through our brain implants or his telepathy. His weird, shifting panther chameleon eyes are level with mine. The food pan in front of Arlo is half-filled with his favorite snack, Cajun-fried gnats. A few tiny gnat legs are still wriggling between his ridged lips as he chews. *Nice.*

Arlo takes a few more chews and then sucks the morsels in with a snap of his sticky tongue. His skin is turning a mottled blue with bands of light green slowly cycling down his body, from head to tail. I can tell from the graphic display that Arlo is upset. Both his eyes swivel forward to focus on me, his human 'partner', his head nodding slowly up and down.

Arlo finally activates his implant so that he can talk to me without using the telepathic powers he acquired when he became a partner.

"Yeah. I thought so too, Jake." Arlo takes a quick lap from the beer in his tray. "When you and I came back from the Karmack incident last week, she had moved to new quarters. She left me a vid." The traveling bands of light green are changing to bright orange and speeding up. Not a good sign.

"She wants us to 'move on', she said. She said it's not anything I did. It's just the way her species handles life in the service. 'No long ties' she said." Arlo snaps up some more gnats and chews angrily. "She said we talked about it when we were slaves on that mining planet in the Q'uaken system, but I'll be damned if I remember that conversation."

Arlo spits out a few legs and slumps on the perch. "I don't get women, Jake. Are you and I really that old fashioned? You gotta help me out, because after all, I got most of my social mores living with you for so long and then sharing that rejuvenation bath. But damn! I really thought Tia and I were in it for the long haul." He slumps a little lower on his perch. "It only lasted for a few months!"

My heart sinks a little, feeling bad for my little buddy. Personal interactions in the FTG and in fact all across the galaxies were still a little mysterious for us. Most of the species we have met so far are not monogamous or polygamous, but spread across a wide range in between. Just keeping up with a single specie's manners and personal expectations keeps me visiting my library AI, Einstein, every other day.

When I'm on board the FTG Triumph, I can access Einstein anytime I need help or access to the ship's data banks. When we joined the FTG, I created Einstein as my 'librarian' avatar so that access to the ship's vast amount of information would be easier. Every crew member has their own avatar and virtual library environment that is configured to provide the crewman with a familiar interface. My environment is a big, dark paneled Victorian den, complete with walls of books, a big chair and ottoman and a full sidebar, stocked with virtual whiskey and cigars.

In affairs of the heart I'm just as confused and befuddled as Arlo. "I'm afraid my stiff necked conservatism has given you a sorry start in this, ummm, shall we say 'liberal' environment?"

Arlo chuckles through his implant, "Liberal? Most of the societies we've run into would make the hippies of the 60's look like a bunch of uptight monks." His sticky tongue zips out and grabs another mouthful of gnats, crunching them slowly. "Don't get me wrong, I understand why. Don't you?"

Slowly swirling my beer on the wet ring under the mug, I can't help thinking about all the differences between our old life and this one. When Arlo and I were 'invited' to join the galactic war I was fat, dumb and not unhappy. I was retired, wasting my life away in my Port Aransas beach house. Deedee, my wife of over forty years, had passed away a few years earlier, taking with her the light from my life. After her death my biggest challenge had been how many brews I could down before breakfast. Arlo was my pet chameleon. His day was like mine, slow, sunbaked and mindless.

Arlo and I were 'recruited' right off the beach by the FTG. Which is to say we were 'this' close to being kidnapped. The Federation of Thirteen Galaxies was in desperate need for recruits with my expertise with Artificial Intelligence and holographic systems. Plus my years as a Nuclear Submariner gave me an ingrained understanding of military discipline and operations. Not that I was your ideal sailor, far from it. My 'creative' approach to problems was not always appreciated. Still, I got the job done and who cares about a couple of Captain's Masts on your record.

I woke up from a nap on the back porch of my beachfront cottage to see three incredibly beautiful women standing in front of me. They had appeared out of nowhere, talking some nonsense about recruiting me. The next thing I knew I was falling into a black void and passed out. When I woke up on the battleship FTG Triumph, Arlo and I were swimming in a fizzing, bubbling bio-tank of rejuvenating 'goop'. It's a technical term. This biotech marvel somehow synced our body's DNA back to our biological prime and enhanced our mental and physical capabilities. So I 'rejuved' back to roughly twenty-five years old, with all my sense heightened and extended. Arlo, like most animal 'partners' who go through the rejuv process, gained sentience and some of my mental baggage in the process. Both of us gained physical and mental abilities, but we're still stuck with Earth's relatively Puritan morals.

Add to the mix the wartime challenges to relationships, inter-species social and physical differences and our need to assimilate vast and intricate cultural mores and you can see the issues we face. My little buddy and I have been behind the relationship eight ball from the beginning and we are pretty slow learners it seems.

"Sure I understand," I say softly. "None of us knows when the next mission will be our last. It's hard enough to create a bond with someone who's not even of your species. You get close and then one of you is shipped off to the other side of the Galaxy or worse." I take a quick swig of my beer and wipe the foam from my mouth with the back of my hand.

"Yeah. Like I said, I understand," snipes Arlo. "That doesn't mean I have to like it, Partner." Arlo flicks his sticky tongue to nab another mouthful of spicy gnats and chews rapidly, his little nostrils puffing out. A quick splash of beer follows the gnats.

"True," I concede. "But it's not all about you or me, Arlo. Tia has a right to live her life as she wants to. She never made any promises to you, did she?" I'm hoping I can make Arlo see it's just the way our lives are now and help him accept it. Arlo can be a bit hard-nosed, both physically and emotionally.

His little eyes do a slow circle, in opposite directions. Sheesh, he does that just to mess with me, I just know it!

"Fine! I can move on if she can, just cool it with the cheesy philosophy." His skin display has cooled down to a uniform sea green with a dark red stripe running down his spine horns.

That's more like my partner. Snarky and proud.

I raise my mug in salute and say, "Here's to my Partner, Arlo the Devastator. Champion of a dozen battles, slayer of Evil Doers across the Galaxies and ladies' man extraordinaire. May his exploits be…"

"If you two are done thumping your virtual chests, the Captain would like a word with you in her ready room."

I look to my side, with my mug still raised. Lieutenant Asa Tillet, or Pixie as I call my girlfriend, is standing in her dazzling white uniform, arms crossed and eyebrows raised.

She leans forward slightly and hooks a thumb to the right. "Now, gentlemen. Let's not keep Captain Starla waiting." A large white and gold transport tile settles behind the lieutenant hovering a few inches off the deck. Without waiting for us to follow, she turns and mounts the tile, grabbing the forward tiller.

Arlo springs up on my shoulder as I move fast to follow Pixie. His little claws dig into my shirt pads and he crouches low as I jump up behind Tillet. The tile's force field takes hold of us as Tillet commands it forward.

These flying tiles are amazing and terrifying. Basically, they are AI controlled hover boards on super-steroids and they are the most efficient way of getting around in the gigantic spaces of the battleship Triumph's innards. They come in all sizes from single person to tiles capable of flinging an entire squadron of Marines at high speed.

I know that the Ship's AI and the tiles are communicating and creating a clear path for us through the labyrinth of the ship's interior, but I can't help but flinch as we careen through the crowds. We're flying over the heads of most of the crew and robots alike, streaking towards the inner cylinder.

Triumph is shaped like a dozen donuts stacked one atop the other. The toroids vary in outer diameter but the interior tube they form is a uniform size throughout the length of the ship. It allows for quick transit area for personnel and cargo from top to bottom. It's also terrifying to fly 'down' or 'up' since there isn't really any 'up' or 'down' while you're whizzing through it, past other tiles flying at break neck speeds in both directions. At any time, there are hundreds of maintenance robos, service robots, supply tiles and crew using the tube access. To me it feels like I'm flowing through a transparent straw with a bunch of supersonic hornets. It seems like a miracle that there are never any collisions.

"What's this about, Lieutenant Sweet Cheeks," pipes up Arlo through our implants.

The tile jukes back and forth a few times in quick succession then does a few barrel rolls, sending my lunch dangerously close to my throat. She snaps around to face us and turns a sharp frown in Arlo's direction. "Excuse me, crewman?"

"Wait, wait, ma'am. Whoa. I was way out of line, I'm sorry. Please excuse me, ma'am." Arlo sounds really contrite and I think I know why.

"Lieutenant Tillet, I believe Arlo is really sorry, ma'am. He's had a recent break up with someone close and it's affected his judgment and his impeccable tack." I'm hoping the humor will keep Arlo out of the brig!

Lieutenant Tillet breaks into grin and laughs out loud. "Impeccable tack? Arlo?" She turns to Arlo and seems to consider something. "Off the record, Arlo, I'm sorry about you and Tia. She came to me before she left and asked me to talk to you. I'm afraid ship's business has kept me from that task. On the record, I'm entering an insubordination demerit to your record." She turns back to the front and adds, "You're better than that, Crewman Arlo. Personal relationships must not interfere with our ability to think and act as a military unit."

Arlo slumps a little lower on my shoulder. "Yes, ma'am. I understand. May I try again?"

Tillet's nod is barely perceptible.

Arlo rises a bit and says, "May we know what's up, ma'am?"

For Arlo, that's as close he gets to acting like a military dude. I'm impressed.

"Ship, privacy channel please."

I can hear a slight click as the Ship's AI redirects us to a private, secure communication channel. "Secure channel engaged, Lieutenant," Ship responds through our implants.

"Thank you, Ship."

Lieutenant Tillet keeps her focus forward as she guides us 'up' towards the bridge. The traffic around us is streaking by. Up, down and zipping into and out of level entrances along the tube. It's impossible to grasp how many tiles are filling the huge cylindrical space. *This would make a great Dali painting.*

"We've had another convoy go missing. The Captain has a plan to find out what's going on. It includes two of our most decorated volunteers. Care to guess who those two crewman are?" She turns slowly to us knowingly, "Two crewman who seem to flaunt military protocol on a regular basis."

Arlo gulps and turns to me. "Sorry, Jake. I think my mouth just got our asses in deep doo doo. Again."

Chapter Three

Pixie puts our tile into a cork-screwing loop before it settles abruptly on the bridge, just behind the Captain's command dais.

Captain Starla is a tall, statuesque Sensanite with flaming red hair and bright emerald eyes. Her humanoid features are accented, rather than muted by her dazzling white uniform. She's always reminded me of those Greek goddess statues in the museums. I found out quickly that her beauty is augmented by a fierce intellect and an almost maniacal professional drive. She's the best Captain in the fleet and a big reason the Triumph excels.

Arlo removes his claws from my shoulder and bobs excitedly. "Yes! Yes! Again! Again!" he shouts through his implant. "That was amazing, Swee.. err, I mean Lieutenant." He lowers his head down on my shoulder and actually looks as contrite as a chameleon with pulsing red skin and yellow eyes can.

"That was close, buddy! Good recovery!" I click through my implant.

"Do you think she bought it?"

"We'll find out soon enough."

Tillet steps off the tile, motioning for us to follow her to stand at attention behind the Captain's platform. In a soft voice she says, "Rest at ease, crewmen, and don't say anything, we're in the middle of a drill."

The bridge is alive with frenetic energy, operators at every station intent on their consoles and the bridge screens. Drill monitors are moving silently between stations, noting operator alertness and actions as the drill progresses.

I knew from the grapevine that Captain Starla would be conducting a weapons exercise today, getting the crew familiar with new systems installed during our last refit. There is no substitute for active drilling, except for actual combat. The Officers and Crew know this and go well beyond the expected training, each shift trying to outdo the others. It's one reason that Triumph has a superior 'Battle E' performance rating.

The forward screens are displaying a coordinated attack from a dozen GHA fighters and a massive Bengal class Destroyer, the equivalent of an FTG heavy Cruiser. Dozens of small enemy fighters are streaking in from every direction like hordes of angry hornets spewing death from laser cannons and blasters. The Destroyer is firing non-stop with torpedoes and plasma cannons. Our shields can't take this beating much longer.

The operator at the weapons console, turns to the XO and reports, "In this phase of the drill the enemy is at 10% power, sir, and firing a full, continuous barrage. The new shields are at 30%, sir, but fading fast. I calculate 45% better resistance to initial contact but a slightly faster fade rate than the old shields."

Captain Starla barely nods at the XO, Lieutenant Commander Betzel, standing to her right. "Continue, XO".

The XO is a Zetazoid from Zeta Prime. Also humanoid, her ever present blonde ponytail is tied up with a small black ribbon that has dark red swords emblazoned on it. Betzel has velvet blue eyes and a smile that could melt titanium. On the few times that I've been on the receiving end of that smile I couldn't help but notice the resemblance to a certain Genic of my youth. There is no smile right now though. The XO's is all business.

The XO says aloud, "Ship, do you concur?"

"Ship" is the generic name for the Triumph's AI, buried deep in the guts of the battleship. Ship monitors virtually everything on board. Operation of the enormous vessel would be impossible without the Artificial Intelligence.

"Ensign Doar is correct, sir. The enhanced shields are able to initially absorb a higher impact from both energy and explosive weapons. They are somewhat slower recovering from a sustained barrage of projectile weapons. Recovery times for beam and plasma weapons is on par with the Revision AAD 22 shield performance."

The Captain seems pleased. It's hard to tell from behind the command chair, but her body language is excited and impressed. I've known the CO and XO long enough to sense their mood. I would have known if the tests did not meet expectations. So would everyone else on the bridge. Starla and Betzel are not shy or hesitant in their praise or their ire. Betzel could stop a four ton stampeding Skegg with single glance.

"Very well, XO. I have a small matter to deal with in my ready room. Program the new weapons drill at 25% and run it a few times. I'll return in twenty. I'll accept your report then." She turns to face the bridge crew and says, "Well done, everyone. Let's shake out the kinks in these systems as quickly as possible. I want at full power drill at 1400 tomorrow. A lot of brass will be watching that drill and I want to come out with our usual superior marks."

Starla comes to attention and says, "XO, you have the bridge."

Betzel snaps to attention. "I relieve you, sir." Turning to the bridge crew, the XO barks crisply, "All right crew, let's reset to the weapons simulation at 25%. Comm, notify the drill squadron to reload and set weapons to 25% of full power. Look sharp, everyone!"

Captain Starla turns towards her ready room and nods to Tillet to follow. *Here we go.*

****

The Ready Room is the Captain's private space to attend to the bazillion administrative details that a Starship demands, while not being on the watch on the bridge. It gives her instant access to the bridge if she is needed but a space to hold conferences and sometimes to just think in private.

The entrance to the Ready Room materializes in front of the Captain just before she strides into the wall. I will never get used to the way room portals seem to melt as you approach and then reappear behind you when you step through. I like the sound of a sliding door or a damn hatch. It creeps me out to watch someone walk through walls like that. The only thing telling you there is a portal there is the outline of the door imprinted on the wall and a marker above it. Every newbie on the ship has been the victim of the bogus door outline prank, me included. Almost broke my nose, but I learned to look for the identification placard above the outline.

Like Captain Starla, this room is crisp, stern and no nonsense. The window across from us is filled with a view of the battle drill surrounding Triumph. 'Enemy' vessels are flying in all directions, firing at our ship in mock battle. It's a dazzling scene, impossible to follow though I know there is an order to the patterns of attack. With a wave of her hand, Starla darkens the window so we won't be distracted.

Part of the near wall is filled with a dozen huge video screens, displaying the ship's operations, systems status, our current position in the quadrant and god knows what else. A two meter transparent 3D holo of the entire battleship is slowly rotating above the far console, thousands of red, blue, green and white dots dispersed everywhere, some fixed and flashing, some moving rapidly, some with blinking, insistent text floating next to them. Tiny red flashing ships are buzzing around Triumph like hornets on a caffeine high.

Once we're all through the portal, Tillet stands at ease and motions for me to do the same. Captain Starla walks to her wall console, sits back on the ledge and crosses her arms. Nobody speaks for a moment. There is an odd tension in my commanding officer. She's not the kind of officer who hesitates for anything.

"What we about to discuss must not leave this room. For any reason, no exceptions. Do you all understand that? Lives depend upon secrecy." Her gaze is somber and intense. This is definitely big. I'm getting that weird tingle along my spine.

I speak first. "You have my word, Captain."

In his John Wayne voice, Arlo pipes in. "Little lady, wild horses couldn't drag it out of me." A stern look from Tillet quickly makes him add, "I mean, you have my word as well, Captain."

Tillet turns back to her commanding officer and nods. "Of course, Ma'am. My word as well."

Captain Starla stands and tugs on her tunic. "I understand this is bit odd and definitely not SOP on Triumph. I think you'll understand why soon enough." She looks at each of us in turn and continues. "There has been a rash of convoy attacks on what are supposed to be secret supply missions. In the last two months we've lost seven convoys. Their cargo is desperately needed in the outer stations. Forty-nine supply ships, four battle tested frigates and three cruisers have been crippled. Most of the crews and civilians have been recovered but there have been causalities and missing personnel. It appears the bandits are after the supplies and seek to keep us engaged with hit and run attacks so that our military vessels cannot return to the front."

The captain looks ready to blow a gasket. "This has got to stop!" Her voice gets higher and louder, finally slamming a fist on the console, sparks flying from the side. I've rarely seen the Captain so worked up. She keeps her emotions on a very short lease.

Blushing deeply, the Captain shakes her head. "I apologize for my outburst. I've lost two close friends to these cowardly attacks. Now I'm afraid I've lost a third, Commander John Sprague." Her shakes a bit. "His convoy missed a mandatory report upon arriving at the delivery point. We suspect the worse and have sent a recon ship to the area."

Tillet starts to touch the Captain's shoulder and pauses. "I'm so sorry, Selenia, I know how close you are to Captain Sprague."

"Yes." She brushes an errant strand of hair aside and smiles. "Thank you, Asa." She shakes her head and straightens again. "This takes us back to you two." A perfectly manicured finger spears Arlo and me. "If you accept it, Fleet Headquarters has given me permission to pursue a covert, embedded mission to find out how these ambushes are happening. I've chosen you two because of you bravery, ability to adapt and frankly your commitment to do whatever it takes to get an operation done by whatever means necessary."

Arlo lowers his head on my shoulder and says, "I told you not to be a hero, numb-nuts. Now see what you've got us into!"

"Hey, I believe you're the one they call 'Arlo the Devastator'! You're the brains in this duo and..."

"OK! We get it. You two have reservations about the assignment." grumbles Tillet. "But consider this. It's a special mission. You could be saving thousands of lives and rounding up a group of bastards that could be waiting to ambush mostly innocent civilians at any time. And think of the outposts that are starving because we can't get supplies through in time. Care to think about it?"

I blush and answer, "No. We don't have to think about. Of course we'll do it. We just like to bitch a little first. It's the Navy way. You know, never volunteer for anything and you might make it to retirement?"

I see the Lieutenant break out in a smile and tilt her head at the Captain. *What's that about?*

Starla chuckles and nods to Tillet. "OK, OK. You win. They accepted in less than a minute. I owe you a round at Twenty Two Forward."

Starla extends a hand for me to shake and says, "Congratulation, crewmen. You are now part of a very deep, undercover operation to find and stop these raids."

I extend my hand and shake her cool, firm hand. Her grip would bring tears to a Wisconsin dairy farmer. It's all I can do keep from wincing.

Arlo raises a forked foot and holds it there. "High two, Cap!" When the Captain raises an eyebrow, he lowers the leg and says, "What? What?" He shakes his little horned head and says, "Too much, Ma'am?" He mutters to me via our implants. "Man, these people need to get the corn cobs out of their..."

"What was that, crewman?" Tillet's voice is icy and stern. "Your implant is not in private mode! Maybe you'd like to spend the night in the brig, practicing basic implant operations?"

The air is definitely frosty until the Captain cracks a smile. "At ease, Arlo. I'd shake your hand if your claws weren't so sharp."

Starla turns and keys up a vid screen on her console. I recognize the star map of the Pesstaa Quadrant. There are hundreds of inhabited systems, circled in green. PIP, my personal moniker for the Ship's AI, is briefing me via my implant as the Captain speaks. Bright icons, spread all across the map are flashing red, the missing crew and cargo listed next to each one.

"Jesus, Captain, I had no idea there were so many incidents. How long as this been going on and why is it being kept secret?"

"We've suspected the coordinated plot for three months, now. But someone is being very clever and not hijacking on a regular basis or in the same areas. As to the secrecy, we don't want the bastards to know we're on to them. Will you enlighten them further, Lieutenant?"

Tillet walks to the vid and starts moving the images around. "These systems were hit first, then more convoys in this area." She touches several icons, expanding them, showing close ups of the planets. "All of these convoys were carrying critical supplies to outposts on the verge of collapse. We're having to divert full squadrons to guard further convoys. It's spreading the fleet thinner at a time when we need every ship in combat."

Captain Starla interrupts, "The salient point is that not only are our outposts suffering, but we're seriously compromising our missions to stop the advance of the GHA. We've lost several planets because we simply don't have enough ships in all the combat areas. We HAVE to find a solution as quickly as possible. That's where you come in."

"Sir?"

Tillet swipes another image onto the vid. It's a huge bizarre mass of ship parts, barges, canisters, girders, cables and old freighters, thrown together haphazardly. It looks like an overmedicated welder went to a giant junk yard and started slapping pieces together.

"This is 'Sewer City', orbiting around Chanana. Headquarters Intel believes at least one of the marauding crews is based there. We hope there is only one, but we can't be sure. They recruit the scum of the galaxy, outfit a new ship and find a way to attach themselves to a convoy. This is where we're sending you."

Behind the floating garbage heap is a dirty brown, desert planet with two small, grayish moons. From the scale of the 'city' against the planet, I'd have to guess it's gigantic, probably miles in diameter. I wonder where the sewage in Sewer City goes. Actually, I don't.

"If it's a known hive of infamy, why haven't we busted in and brought them to justice?

"The FTG doesn't interfere with local law enforcement and politics, you know that. Sewer City is actually a legitimate, functioning trade depot and crucial to the local planet economies. We believe the saboteurs operate deep within the city, hidden from sight. Probably paying off officials to remain anonymous."

"OooKaay. You're going to send Arlo and me to a sector of the Galaxy where every thug and pirate uses a picture of Arlo as a knife target. That's the sector of space where Arlo destroyed the Haknak family drug ring and put half of them in prison for life. Why don't you just smear us with butter and toss us into a cell with some starving porcupines!"

Arlo turns slowly and gives me the twirling evil eyes. "Starving porcupines?? Butter??"

"Sorry, it just popped into my head! Damn." I gather back my wits, few that they are and say, "Any idea how we stay alive for more than ten seconds once we show our faces?"

"Yes," says the Captain, "we're going to disguise you, of course."

I can sense Arlo's confusion through our telepathic link. This is raising all sorts of tingly red flags for me too.

Arlo beats me to the obvious question. "Um, sir. How 'exactly' could you disguise a lizard and an ugly bag of bones? Our faces are plastered all over the 'Bad Guys Weekly Gazette's wanted pages. A little makeup and a wig isn't going to go very far, you know. Though I must say I would rock the whole wig thing."

Lieutenant Tillet smiles and says, "Of course not, Arlo. We don't want there to be any chance you'll be recognized." She puts a pink fingernail lightly on his little snout. "We're going to bio-morph you. Both of you. You'll be unrecognizable."

"Uh, bio-morph?" I stutter. This sounds bad. I don't want to be bio-anythinged! "You're going to change our appearance by changing our bodies? Please tell me it's just some costume or armor."

"Yeah," spouts Arlo. "I'm too small to bio-dorph, right?"

Captain Starla shakes her head. "It's 'bio-morph', Arlo. And yes, you are small. But we can still alter your DNA to make you larger or smaller, with just about any body structure changes your DNA can handle. We will have to determine just what you can tolerate first and then decide the best bio-morph for this assignment. There are a few caveats though."

Crap! There is always caveats in these things.

"OK, let's have it Ma'am. Give it to us straight. Arlo can take it." Arlo gives the back of my head a sharp snap with his tail. "Ouch! OK, OK. WE can take it."

Tillet's pretty eyebrows crinkle a little in concern. "You won't be able to return to your normal biology for some time and you'll have to return here to do it. The process has to be reversed in the same lab it started. Even then there is a chance it cannot be reversed at all. A very small chance, but it's possible."

"You mean we could be stuck as these bio-dorks forever?" gulps Arlo. I was thinking the same thing. This is sounding less and less cool. I really like my current body, just as it is.

Captain Starla nods and says, "That's right gentlemen. But that's just a small issue in this mission. There are much greater chances for things to go wrong."

"If this is a pep talk, Ma'am, you need to spice it up at little. Is there any chance that things could go right? Like, you know, we find the bad guys, take 'em out and return home in time for breakfast?" I'd rather joke about these things than run screaming from the room. Barely.

Arlo tries to cover his nerves just like me, but I can tell from his emphatic link that he's not happy. "Excuse me, Captain, but could you be a little more specific about the mess we just volunteered for? Is it the D'bak? The Marphka? Some other freakin' dysfunctional mercenary family?"

The D'bak, literally 'Blood Family', and the Marphka are aligned with the GHA Hegemony of mercenaries, pirates and all around bad guys. The GHA hire them to harass and disrupt the FTG's efforts to stop the advance of the aquaforming. The 'Families' vie for dominance and the spoils of the war. Arlo and I have had several run-ins with the families, most ending with some really pissed off or violently deceased family members.

Starla dips her head and looks to the side. "No. I'm afraid Intel has identified the king pin on Sewer City to be Captain Ryan G'radian, an Un-Jun." In a lower voice, she continues. "In any war there are mistakes. Some worse than others."

I've never seen the Captain like this. Vulnerable and embarrassed.

Tillet steps close to Starla and puts a hand lightly on her shoulder. "Let me explain, Selenia."

Tillet turns to us and says, "Captain Starla was fresh out of the Academy and assigned as an Engineering Lieutenant onboard the 'Eleusis', a cruiser in quadrant 8311-XHT. Their mission was to investigate a suspected mercenary terror cell on one of the moons of Beamor. The intel came from a supposedly reliable source on Beamor. The source said that the cell was heavily armed, dangerous and preparing to attack a nearby FTG outpost."

Captain Starla motions to Tillet to stop. "Tillet is right. The Captain of the Eleusis believed that the cell would inflict heavy damage on our troops at the outpost. So we went in with lasers blazing. It was over in minutes. There was no resistance. No fight at all. We had decimated the area around the suspected cell."

Oh no. "It wasn't a terror cell, was it?"

Tillet continued, "No. They were traders, not terrorists. The source on Beamor was a trading competitor. They fed us bogus intel and then stood back while we destroyed their rivals. It worked. Eleusis quickly determined they had been duped and sent down emergency medical help. It was too late. Over a hundred innocent people were dead. Whole families."

Starla and Tillet pause, each with their own memories. I can hear Arlo in my head. "That would kill me, Jake. I can't imagine how the Captain feels."

We give Starla a moment to recover. She shakes her head, her mouth pulled thin and tight. This lady has an iron will.

"There is no excuse for the debacle. The Captain was over zealous, eager to strike a blow to the enemy and get revenge for attacks on local outputs made by other forces. Instead, they committed a horrendous act of terrorism themselves."

"How does that tie in with this mission, Ma'am?" I said.

Captain Starla stiffens her back and smooths her tunic. "One of the families killed in that raid was G'radian's. His mother, wife and three daughters. Only G'radian and his son, who were away on a trading junket, survived. So you can imagine why G'radian has no love for the FTG. And that's one reason this mission is so risky. If G'radian believes you to be FTG, it won't go well for you."

"I can't say I blame him, Ma'am. If that happened to my family, I'd move Heaven and Earth to find those responsible. I'm not normally a revenge kind of guy, but that might push me over the edge."

Tillet nods, "I understand, Jake. I've lost family members in this infernal conflict as well. Captain G'radian has done exactly that. He's tracked down most of the bridge crew from the Eleusis."

Arlo gulps. "Did he kill them?"

"No, he did not. That's what makes us believe there is still something honorable in him. Instead of killing them, he abducted them. He left messages that he sold them to slavers. A fate he feels is better than they deserve."

Arlo says nervously, "This is feeling less like a party and more like a freakin' nightmare! And Jake and I are going to be knee deep in do-do before it's over. Is there anything else we need to know? You know, like this Captain Grr-whatever likes lizard stew?"

The Captain and Tillet exchange glances. Tillet turns to us and says. "Now that you mention it, there is a small 'issue' you'll need to work with. We will have to remove your implants. They will most certainly deep scan you and discover them. Which would end your mission before it gets started."

"What?" Arlo shouts. "You want us to enter enemy territory without any way to communicate or contact the good guys. Are you nuts?" I can feel his anger and fear.

"Relax little buddy, you can still use your telepathy to talk to me." I give Captain Starla the evil eye, "He's right, this would cut us off from any hope of rescue if something goes wrong."

"Yes, I know. You can withdraw from the assignment and no one will think less of either of you. It's an incredible risk you'll be taking."

"Hey, nobody said anything about turning tail, lady. We're just putting all the cards on the table so we can look at our hand." Arlo is up on his legs and positively quivering. "Jake and I have never let you down. Right, partner?"

My little buddy is John Wayne, Rambo and James Bond, all rolled up in a multicolored lizard suit. Size 002.

"That's right, my friend. Now that we know the whole story..." I give Tillet some raised eyebrows just in case there is more. She shakes her head no. "We won't fail you, Captain. Let's get this party started!"

Chapter Four

The Un-Jun trading vessel 'Tau' squats at the far end of a docking bay hidden in the metallic folds of Sewer City's underbelly. Chosen for its concealed location, the bay serves as the base for a mishmash group of mercenary ships and crews led by Captain Ryan G'radian, an Un-Jun.

Tau's once proud bright green hull is now faded and dull. Its sides are scored from neglect and scrapes with the FTG convoys he's tangled with. The ship is a common trader configuration, basically a big rectangular box, sixty meters long, sixty meters wide and fifteen meters tall, with a smaller box of a cockpit attached to the front. Allowing for space for the crew of two's needs and the ship's engine and machinery it's still large enough to carry over four hundred tons of cargo. The Tau's sole armament is a pair of blaster turrets under the cockpit for 'defense'. The shields have been upgraded but wouldn't do much good in a prolonged firefight. The ship is a hauler, not a fighter.

G'radian is sitting in the pilot's chair savoring his morning cup of garl, a bitter brew made from the ground roots of the garl plant, native to his home world. Beside him, Bolton, his son, is standing just in front of the co-pilots chair, keeping a wary eye on G'radian's mercenary Lieutenant, Krmot, a 'Snsh'. Krmot is large for his species at almost five feet from tail to snout. His hide is dark green with muddy, mottled brown patches. His large back haunches and legs allow him to stand on taloned feet, balancing on his short, stubby tail. Large alligator-like eyes, with dirty, dark yellow pupils, perch on top of his ridged head. Rows of serrated teeth protrude at all angles from his drooling, angular mouth. A ragged double row of six inch, dark red and black plates protrude out from his spine from head to tail. Some of the plates have been torn from the flesh, others have been chewed in half.

"I need to do some recruiting to bring my ship back to fighting strength, Cap. And I could use some extra credits to buy a better class of crewmen this time." Krmot's reptilian eyes continually rotate, glancing nervously between the two Un-Jun's. He never knows when Captain G'radian's mood will send him off on a rage. Best not to be too close, just in case. It hasn't escaped his notice that Bolton has hand resting on his blaster holster. Krmot fears and hates them both, but they pay well and don't ask too many questions about his methods.

"Our ships have lost twenty crewmen to desertion and another ten to brawls in the bars. Some of the ships are running skeleton crews." He shifts slowly back and forth, watching the brooding figure. "What do you want me to do, Cap?"

Captain Ryan G'radian looks up from his stone mug, dark eyes just visible under his large brimmed hat. Small bone ridges protrude above the Un-Jun's eyes. The serrated ridges line both cheeks and across his broad chin. The white bone is a glaring contrast to his dark olive skin. Intricate blue clan tattoos have been carved into the exposed bones and his skin, making his face both terrifying and mesmerizing.

He considers spacing this worthless creature for his stupidity. There's no excuse for allowing crewmen to escape or die senselessly in the bars of this cesspit of a trade colony, even if they are mercenaries. He can sense Bolton's anger as well, his son's stance stiffening at the news.

But he's received intelligence from his spy network that the Federation is getting another supply convoy ready, and he wants a ship planted before it leaves. The spy he inserted into their headquarters has paid for his 'fees' many times over. G'radian's not sure how much longer the spy can stay undiscovered, so he's stepping up his attacks. There are only two more officers to find before he can rest from his vendetta.

He reaches into a side pocket of his full length, deep blue arn-skin cloak and extracts a small pouch. The bag, full of gold credits, rises and falls a few inches above his bony, taloned hand as Captain G'radian contemplates his next move. He knows this slime bag is skimming the credits, but what choice does he have? Time to put the fear of Gouk, the Un-Jun god of War, into this worm.

Captain G'radian sets the cup on a console and rises slowly from his chair, eyes smoldering, face rigid and stony. Bolton starts forward as well, but G'radian motions for his son to stand fast. He steps towards the quivering creature, towering over it. He snaps his arm up at the elbow and a bright green, meter long phasing-saber instantly appears in his hand. The edges of the sword are alive with dancing white and green lightning, crackling and sizzling like a living thing.

Krmot takes a short step back in shock. He knows it's too late to run, that saber would slice him in two before he got halfway turned around. He raises his fore-arms in defense. "Cap! Cap! Wait. What did I do? There ain't no need for that!" His whole body starts to tremble.

Captain G'radian stops just short of the poor Snsh and brings the hissing sword to within an inch of the scaly snout. He tosses the pouch in the air and lowers the sword. Krmot just manages to snag the bag before it hits the floor.

"This is your last chance to impress me, Krmot. If you can't get a decent crew and have those garbage heaps of your squad ready by the time I need you, I'm going to take another chunk of that fat tail of yours and use it for fish bait. Then I'm going to find myself a new Lieutenant and fleet to carry out these raids. A first mate who knows how to follow my orders. Disable the ships and take the cargo. Bring the FTG officers on my list back to me. That's it, nothing more!"

"Yes, Cap, yes sir! I won't let you down." *You bastard. If you didn't pay so well, I'd leave you to rot in your skin.* "How soon do you think I'll be shipping out, if I can ask."

"You'll know when I tell you. Just have your ship ready to insert as soon as possible. Make sure your mates understand my orders on the raid. And one more thing, 'Captain'," says G'radian sarcastically.

Krmot sits back on his tail a little further, too afraid ask.

G'radian raises the phasing-saber one more time. "If you steal from me again, you're going to missing more than a bit of skin."

Krmot nods rapidly and then spins on his tail and scuttles out of the chamber, eager to get away. *Damn you, G'radian! Someday you're going to push someone too far and get what's coming to you.* He disappears out the ship's open access ramp like his tail was on fire.

The sizzling sword slices back and forth through the air, humming wildly. G'radian chants a mantra a few times to calm himself. Fighting to regain control of his anger, G'radian finally sighs heavily. The lightning playing along the sword flutters and dies. With a snap of his wrist, it draws back into its sheath inside the sleeve. He shrugs his cloak back into place completely covering the weapon.

Bolton glances at his father and mutters as he leans against the bulkhead, "I trust him about as far as I can spit, Father."

"Captain, you have a message on a secure channel." The voice of his ship's AI hums from the cockpit intercom. "Should I patch it through?"

"We'll take it in my quarters, Ship, patch it through in private mode." He sweeps off the chair, cloak billowing behind him, and makes for the small living quarters that doubles as a command ready room. Bolton strides behind him, eager to hear the intel. He thumbs the control to raise the ramp and close and lock the cargo hatch so they won't be interrupted.

****

G'radian palms the portal open and steps to the small desk, next to the Captain's cot. The room is spartan, like its owner. The bed, desk and tiny bathroom with shower is all that G'radian needs and wants. He shares the space with his son on long voyages, alternating watches. While on Sewer City, he spends little time in his room, preferring to be hands-on with all the day-to-day tasks of running his tiny enterprise. His small fleet of haulers and fighters wonder when he ever sleeps, always keeping an eye out for the boss and his son. None slack on the job, fearing one of the two will catch them at it and rip them a new one.

"Let's see what's so damn important." Ryan thumbs the lock on a panel on his desk and it slides to one side, revealing a full military grade communication system. Keying the private com system he says, "Talk to me."

The response is faint and warbles in and out as the system struggles to keep the connection. "Two convoys scheduled in next three weeks. Coordinates to follow." There is a short spurt of static and then then line goes dead. The comm systems analyze the static and display the results as a fifty centimeter 3D stellar map. The image spins into focus, two pulsing red dots near the center showing where the convoys will transit. Floating next to each is a date and information about the convoys.

Captain G'radian studies the map, using his fingers to move the display around to examine it from all directions. "Well, my Federation targets, where are you going this time? Where do I send my ships to cause you the most pain? What outpost can I strangle to make you scream as I did?"

Bolton steps up to the map and says, "Ship, plot the possible destinations from these two starting coordinates. Target FTG outposts that are known to be requesting resupply."

Ryan nods his approval at this tactic. "Good idea, son. That should narrow the search."

The map shifts and rotates. "Here are the most likely destinations, considering all factors." The AI adds white lines to connect the starting red dots with five pulsing blue squares. Two lines flow from one of the starting points to destinations in close proximity to each other. Three lines trace from the other red dot to the remaining blue dots.

"Damn! I don't have enough ships to cover that many routes. Ship, show the two targets that are the most distant from the starting points. Assume that those are the outposts that are in most need of resupply."

Instantly the display has only two lines, one from each red dot to one blue dot. "These appear to be the most likely routes, sir, based on those parameters."

Bolton's says excitedly, "Magnify each route, ship. Show any FTG posts along their path."

G'radian nods again. Though he and his son often disagree on Ryan's relentless vendetta to avenge his family and tribe, Bolton always has his back. His son is showing traits that will make him an excellent leader and trader. Ryan cringes a little inside as he ponders for the thousandth time if it is time to take his son's advice and return to honest trading. What was once an all-consuming, burning rage to revenge his family's death has become instead a sharp, cold stone wedged deeply in his chest. Always there. Always painful.

The routes are each sprinkled with white dots along the way. The path to Ryan's right has five white dots, the one on his left has only one outpost, situated near the middle of the route.

Captain G'radian slaps a hand on the desk and shouts, "Yes! I've got you!" He gestures to zoom in on the outpost on the left. It becomes a bright blue, green and brown planet with three moons. The planetary oceans and land masses are clearly visible beneath wispy white clouds. Text floats next to each mass. Planet 'Dendar's type, population, and other specifics are shown in a scrolling list.

"Dendar." He waves the display away with a hand signal. "Ship, start plotting an intercept course for Krmot's ship so that he will be in place when I give the word. Give him the latest security codes and falsify a manifest of energy crystals and medical supplies."

"Yes, sir. Shall I notify him when we get the exact date and time of the departure?"

"No. Let me know as soon as you get the information. I'll contact him myself."

He turns his head to Bolton, jabs a threatening finger in the air and says, "I want to convince Krmot not to fail me again."

Chapter Five

Arlo and I are taking in a beer and burger in crew's lounge Twenty-Two, our regular hangout. The place is packed. The second watch has just been relieved and the off going crew scrambles for some food and relaxation before heading off to other duties. There is always maintenance to perform, drills or training to attend. There is rarely a 'free' minute in a spacer's life onboard a fighting ship like Triumph.

Crewmen of all species are mingling together, laughing, talking, squeaking and croaking over an amazing assortment of foods. The smells are, hmm, let's go with intoxicating. At the next table, there is a bowl of some small, orange, spiky spider-looking morsels struggling mightily to not be dinner, but to no avail. They disappear quickly into the maw of a hungry Grockna. Grockna have always reminded me of those Rock'em Sock'em robot toys, square and granite solid. Except Grockna's are seven feet tall and have a hide that would make a shark envious. The crewman quickly washes them down with a steaming mug of something that looks like lumpy mud. Ick. Just damn ick.

"Are we nuts, Jake?" Arlo says through his implant, interrupting my lunch voyeurism. He's chowing down on some kind of wriggling blue worms that have dozens of tiny green eyes at both ends. *Yuck, that is just gross!* "We're about to dive into a bubbling vat of mucus and let Nanel's bio-geeks mess with our DNA. What if it doesn't work? What if I come out looking like you!? This could be a disaster! I don't want to spend forever looking like a lumpy bag of bones with a bad haircut."

"Hey, who you calling lumpy, peewee? Relax, partner, Lieutenant Commander Nanel's team has run the simulations a dozen times, just to make sure our bodies can take the bio-morph. She is not going to take chances with us. Besides, she got a little crush on you, and you know it." It's a running joke of unrequited love between the Ship's Surgeon, Lieutenant Commander Nanel, and Arlo. Nanel is a statuesque Andrian. The race of bio-android humanoids joined the war eons ago, after their world was almost aquaformed by the GHA and its mercenaries.

Arlo rises on his little legs and smiles. Or at least what passes for a smile for a chameleon with a ridged mouth. In his best Sean Connery voice he slurs, "It's a cross I have to bear, Gigantor. She's a sucker for a handsome, debonair hero like myself. Can't say I blame her." He whips his tail back and forth and settles back on his perch.

I'm about to take another sip of my beer and try to come up with a snarky response when the attention bell sounds in my implant. Arlo's head snaps up, so I know he hears it too. "Crewmen Jake Jasper and Arlo, report to Medical Laboratory Forty-Two, immediately. Medical Lab Forty-Two. Acknowledge, please."

Arlo jumps on it. "Acknowledged, Ship, we're on our way."

A transport tile zips into the room above our heads and settles quickly to the deck next to us. I grab my little buddy, sit him on my shoulder pad and hop onto the tile. The tile's static field grips us and the tile rises rapidly back to within inches of the ceiling before zipping out of Twenty-Two.

I trigger my implant and say, "PIP, thanks for the quick transport. We're up and away. We just ate so please keep the acrobatics to a minimum!"

As soon as I say it I know it's the wrong thing to say to PIP, who has a wicked sense of humor for an AI. The tile flips upside down, putting my head inches above the diners, some of who are seven feet tall. The tile bounces up and down skimming above or around everyone at literally break-neck speed. A plate of steaming spaghetti, I think, whizzes by my head from a pissed off crewman.

"Sorry! Sorry! Sorry! Hey, PIP, knock it off!"

The tile suddenly rights itself and speeds on to the center of the ship. I've got to have a heart to bio-matrix talk with PIP someday.

*****

The medical laboratory is vacant except for Arlo, me, Nanel and Pixie. Medical facilities are usually little bee hives of activity, but the usual lab techs and nurses milling around the consoles are nowhere to be seen. It's eerily quiet. I can feel Arlo's nervousness too. Our telepathic link goes into full empathy mode when Arlo is stressed.

I didn't even know this lab existed. That's not so unusual considering the sheer number of compartments on Triumph and my modest pay grade, but I have a feeling that this place isn't known by a lot of people no matter what their clearance. The tile that brought us here made lots of twists and turns inside some empty corridors of this level.

These labs are amazing. I keep wondering if the modelers for some TV series somehow stole the cool touch screens from these ships or vice versa. Come to think of it, the FTG has recruited from Earth lots of times. I wonder...

"Heads up, Pilgrim," barks Arlo in my head using his best John Wayne voice. "The Captain just walked in. I think we're about to be bio-duped".

Captain Starla steps to the center of the consoles, leans back and folds her arms. She fixes us with those emerald green eyes and says, "Alright crewmen, this is your last chance to reconsider this mission. Once you are bio-morphed you'll be sequestered here while you adapt to your new bodies. We're hoping you'll be ready to go in two weeks. At that point we'll insert you into the Sewer City underworld where you'll be on your own."

"We have considered it, Ma'am. Arlo and I know the score and we're ready to proceed." Arlo nods his excitement on my shoulder pad.

"Let's get this done, Ma'am. Have you found the best bio-weenie changes for us? Is it too late to ask about being a pirate with one eye? You know. I could be Captain Jack and Jake could be my pet monkey? Arrrgghhhh!" Drool drips from his jaws onto my shoulder pad.

"Hey, knock it off, Captain Peewee, this is a new uniform!"

Captain Starla holds up a hand for peace. "Time to get serious, you two. I'm extremely proud of you. The FTG is proud of you, even though no one else may ever know about this. We have to keep this secret between us. It may be a useful tactic in the future." She nods to Lieutenant Commander Nanel. "Commander, would you please walk us through this procedure and give our volunteers a quick look at the models you've created?"

Nanel unfolds her arms and turns to a console. A meter high 3D hologram spins into life above the console. At its center is a model of me and Arlo, sans clothes for me, showing all my manliness.

"Really, you couldn't model a t-shirt and Hawaiian shorts for me? Sheesh!"

Nanel gestures over the console and my model has on a pair of neon green shorts and a t-shirt with lime green parrots and lush lavender flowers. "There. Is that better?" She chuckles and shakes her head. "I'll never understand the human sense of embarrassment about nudity. You have a wonderful, athletic body. Why be ashamed of it?"

"Well, uh. It's not easy overcoming a lifetime of Puritan morals, Ma'am. Besides, I'd like to point out that we're not the only ones with some odd cultural habits. I believe your society frowns on reciting poems and singing in public? What's up with that?"

I swear Nanel blushes and looks down. "Touché, Jake. We consider singing and poetry to be an extremely personal act between two lovers, and not acceptable for public display."

The Captain utters a soft cough. "Can we save the cultural norms discussions for a later date, people? Commander, please proceed."

Nanel nods and turns again to the console. A few beeps and whistles later and the models slowly morph into our altered forms, Arlo's first, mine fading into the background.

Arlo's slim, sixty centimeter long chameleon body starts to expand, end to end, until it's almost five feet from stem to stern. Little buds sprout half way between the front and back legs and slowly grow into another set of legs. All six feet lose their bifurcated claws, the back four become raptor-like taloned feet, each with three nasty looking daggers extending from leathery sheaths. The front two sprout three fingers and two opposing thumbs on muscular arms and shoulders.

The legs and torso are bulking up with rippling muscles. The head flattens, becoming round, ridged and spiked like a Texas horned-toad. A chin develops from the jaw. A long, yellow, forked tongue flicks in and out. The eyes stay on the sides of the head and keep their weird shape and independent movement. A series of short reddish brown spikes circle the long neck, looking like a vicious pit bull's collar.

"Holy crap, Jake, look at that! I'm gonna be the Horny-Toad Hulk! Look at those toe nails. I'll bet I'll able to slice and dice my way through a herd of rhinos." Arlo tilts his head, looking closer at the model. "Hey, wait. Ma'am, that sure looks like a noble chin and all but do I detect something different about the mouth?"

Nanel smiles proudly. "That's right, Arlo. You're going to have vocal chords. You should be able to speak aloud. I worked hard to find the right gene modification so that you can talk. You're going to need that ability to interact with the mercenaries without giving away that you're telepathic. Hopefully the Ship's training routines will be able to bring you up to speed quickly."

"Hear that, Jake me Buckoo? Pretty soon we'll be able to sling pithy insults at each other and everyone can hear them. The Universe will be in balance again."

Great, just what I need. "Super-duper, buddy. Can't wait to hear what voice comes out of your new vocal chords."

Nanel holds up a hand and says, "Let's see how Jake's model turned out. I hope you like it, I worked ready hard to make you look ferocious and formidable. It's roughly based on one of the most terrifying beasts on the jungle planet 'Grulaatec'. You'll need a physically commanding form to merge into their culture as Arlo's combat slave. I believe your term would be 'kick-ass'."

Yes! Now we're cookin' with Crisco. "Yes, that's it. Great, Ma'am."

Arlo's model shifts to the rear of the display and my avatar moves forward. As it does it starts to morph, shedding the clothes. My legs become thick haunches and my butt drops to the floor. A muscled torso extends up to a thick neck and large triangular head with long pointed ears. My arms are attached to broad shoulders but are kinda short. My hands have four fingers and are tipped with nasty, black, pointed claws.

The mouth splits my face, almost ear to ear and has several rows of sharp pointed teeth. Two large buck teeth extending like fangs half way down my chin. My skin is hairless, wrinkled and pink. My body is…

Oh crap. I look like...

Arlo's voice cackles maniacally though the implant. "Oh my God, Jake, you're going to be a giant, pink bunny rabbit! Waaaaahaahaaaaaa!"

Chapter Six

Strantos' bridge is in chaos, bodies and equipment strewn everywhere, at insane angles. Dark gray smoke is roiling from the forward consoles. Most of the bridge lights have failed, giving the scene a hellish hue as the red emergency lights sputter on and off and console graphics glow in the smoke.

Eva J'Kal swims slowly up from the murky dark waters of her unconscious mind to the flickering lights behind her eyelids. Soft sounds are becoming louder and sharper, changing from soft bells to clanging alarms, piercing like needles into her mind. There is a metallic taste in her mouth and something warm dripping from her nose and down her brow. Pain flashes through her right wrist, up her arm to the shoulder. She cries out, gasping and choking.

J'Kal summons all her will and forces her eyes open. The harsh flashing red light bathes the room, pulsing in time with the loudest alarm. The acrid smoke assails her, stinging her nose and eyes. She heaves several times, feeling like she going to cough up a lung. It's hot and getting hotter.

"Eva! Eva!" A shadowy form kneels over her, moving close to her face, the voice strangely muffled. "Eva, wake up. Get to your feet, we need to get to an evac pod, now!" The dim face suddenly pops into focus. "Captain. Wha…"

"No time for this now, Eva, we have to get to a pod. I've already sent the surviving bridge crew to their pods. Come on, Eva, NOW!" Command Sprague grabs his XO's shoulder. She screams in agony. "Sorry, but we have to go." He grabs the other arm and drags her to her feet, moving towards the last remaining escape capsule behind his chair.

"John Boy, is everyone off the ship?"

"All remaining survivors, with the exception of you and Lieutenant J'Kal, have abandoned ship, sir. You must leave now, there is another wave of fighters approaching. Our shields have failed and engines are offline. Strantos is defenseless."

Sprague palms the pod door and shoves J'Kal in head first. He jumps in and slams the door closed, spinning immediately to the pod chair and slapping the emergency launch pad before he or J'Kal are even in their harnesses. The pod explodes through the bridge tunnel and out into space at full speed, driving the two crewman into a heap against the aft bulkhead. Sprague groans, hoping he didn't break bones. He struggles to his feet and drags J'Kal into a mesh cargo web to keep her stable. He moves forward to the pilot's chair and takes control of the pod.

"John Boy, we're clear. Is there any way you can maneuver or fold out of here before they return?" Sprague already knows the answer, but his bond with John Boy goes deeper than the usual AI relationship. AI's aren't supposed to have souls even though some are sentient. John Boy is like family to Sprague.

"No sir, there is nothing I can do to save myself or Strantos. I'm sorry, sir. I realize what must be done."

The Captain nods, he knows also. "Initiate scuttle protocol, John Boy, there are too many civilian ships in the area to self-destruct. You have served above and beyond. You will be missed."

"Thank you, sir. It has been an honor...." The voice of the AI halts in mid-sentence. Sprague looks out the aft viewer. The Stranto's exterior lights are being extinguished, one by one. A second after the last light goes dark the ship shudders and cracks into pieces, like a pair of giant hands crushed it, large pieces of the ship slowly drifting apart. Strantos is dead.

"Damn!" John Sprague's anger starts to well up at the loss of his ship, crew and John Boy. He slams a fist on the chair arm and screams his frustration. "Cowards and thugs! You bastards are going to pay!"

A groan from his lieutenant brings him back to his senses. He shakes off his anger to deal with the immediate problems. He checks the sensors for his crew's pod identification markers, convoy markers and for enemy ships. "All pods, Strantos Prime, report in and then head for the rendezvous point on the planet." Keeping one ear open for the responses, he walks back to the straps keeping J'Kal from flying around the pod.

"Blue One, four crewmen."

"Yellow Five, three crewmen."

Sprague lets his mind absorb the reports while he examines J'Kal. She's entangled in the restraining straps, unconscious but stirring. He grabs the med kit, finds the analyzer and scans her from head to toe. The scanner whirs and bleeps and says, "Patient has a mild concussion, a fractured right wrist, heavy bruising to face and legs and possible internal bleeding. Please apply the needle to her neck for a stabilizing injection and seek medical help immediately."

"No kidding. I'll just buzz over to the closest hospital." He presses the device's pointed tip to J'Kal jugular, injecting pain meds and a concoction to stabilize her internal bleeding. Carefully untangling his semi-conscious friend from the harness, he gently guides her to the co-pilots chair. He straps her into the chair and goes back to the first-aid kit. He extracts a small splint and applies it to her right wrist, the foam gently encircling the limb and then hardening to hold it stable. He checks her eyes and breathing and decides that will have to do for now.

He needs to get a grip on his charges quickly. He says, "Ship, give me a sit-rep."

The pod's AI, though limited, is capable of monitoring the situation inside the cabin as well as outside. "All known crew pods have reported, sir. There are two hundred fifty six survivors. All pods are on course for the rendezvous point. I estimate forty minutes until all pods have landed."

"Very good, Ship. Can you survey the area for any enemy ships?"

"It appears that all undamaged convoy and enemy ships have transited from the area. The only remaining vessels are escape pods from Strantos and the remains of two convoy ships. There are no signs of life on the convoy ships."

"Who is the highest ranking bridge officer in the other pods?"

"There are no surviving bridge officers except for you and Lieutenant J'Kal. Engineering Division Officer, Lieutenant Junior Grade Connor is the next ranking officer. He is currently in pod Red Eleven."

Oh my God, I've lost my bridge and most of my crew! Sprague pauses a moment as the enormity of this waves over him. I can grieve later, I have to get everyone to safety in case the bastards return. "Ship, inform JG Connor to coordinate the evac to the planet. Inform me when we are five minutes out. Make sure he acknowledges his orders."

"Yes, sir." A moment later it reports, "Orders have been acknowledged, sir."

Sprague turns his attention back to J'Kal. He kneels and pats her good hand. "Eva. Eva. Please wake up. I'm going to need you by my side if we're going to get through this." He continues to rub her hand and will his XO back to consciousness.

J'Kal moans and sways side to side in the chair, her pale face slowly regaining its normal pallor. Finally, her eyes flutter and open. She looks down at her soft cast, not sure what is on her arm. She utters a soft cry as the pain shoots up her arm. The pain pulls her completely awake, eyes wide open. She scans the view screen ahead, the planet almost filling the screen, then turns to her Captain.

"What the hell happened, sir? I remember coming out of transit and then all hell broke loose on the bridge. I was trying to get to the weapons console when I blacked out."

"I'll fill you in more after we get what's left of my crew to the surface." His voice is low and sad. "We lost over seven hundred crewmen in less than twenty seconds. It was an ambush. There must have been twenty mercenaries waiting for us. I didn't see any GHA ships, but I didn't have time to scan. They were waiting for us, Eva."

"How? How could they possibly know our destination? The crew... seven hundred? Sweet Galla in Heaven." She shakes her head in disbelief. "Why would they destroy Strantos? Why murder the crew? That many ships could have disabled Strantos and taken the cargo ships without any loss of life! We would have had to surrender!"

"I've been wondering the same thing. It doesn't make sense." He examines her arm and checks her eyes again. "The med-kit says you have a mild concussion and a fractured wrist. You have some internal bleeding but it's been stabilized for now. We need to get you to a hospital as soon as possible."

He sits back in the pilot's chair and says, "I need to get a status update." He keys the pod's comm unit. "Connor, this is Sprague, what's our status?"

"We've lost three pods from Strantos, sir. They could not evade the debris and secondary explosions. All remaining pods, including yours, are on course for the rendezvous landing. The survivor count so far is two hundred and forty-nine. I am trying to establish contact with each of the convoy's escape pods, but at this point the total count is unknown."

"Give the estimate you have so far, Lieutenant. Just the survivor count."

There was a hesitation. Sprague could hear a conversation between Connor and another crewman. "Our current count is three hundred twenty-seven. We have only been able to contact the escape pods of nine of the convoy's twenty-one vessels. Everyone we've contacted is headed for the rendezvous point."

"Very well. Continue to make contact with those pods. How long before we make planet fall?" He could have found out from his AI, but Sprague wanted to keep Connor focused and engaged.

"All known pods should be planet side in seven minutes, sir. I have assigned a team to set up a base camp. We'll attend to the injured and try to set up communications with the closest facilities. It appears that we'll be less than twenty-six kilometers from the city of Tanadoc. I have Lieutenant Shurtz coordinating our landing with the convoy pods."

"Excellent, Connor. Set up a location beacon. We will join you soon. Strantos..." He chokes back a gasp as he realizes that Strantos was gone. "Sprague out."

*****

An hour later Connor and Shurtz have set up a base, inspected the pods and set up a temporary field hospital from parts and pieces of all the landing pods. Sprague and J'Kal are finishing up a tour, with Connor in tow.

As they walk past the hospital entrance, a tall, white haired man marches towards them. His smock is stained with a disturbing mixture of dark burgundy dried and bright red fresh blood. His eyes are blazing, his fists clenched in fury. Lieutenant Commander John Tilley stops in front of Captain Sprague, his bristling eyebrows raised in question. "What in God's name happened, Captain? We've got dead and wounded everywhere." He glances up to the sky and points an accusing finger. "I can't even guess how many died up there or on their way down here! This was a supply convoy, not a military mission. What the hell happened?" Tilley steps back a bit to gain control of himself. "This is madness," he says quietly. "Madness."

Sprague puts his hand on the doctor's soiled shoulder and looks directly into the eyes of the Strantos' Chief Medical Officer and friend. "I know, Doc, I know." He has no words to explain or comfort his friend. "Do what you can. I promise you, we won't stop until we find the answer." He drops his hand and asks, "Do you need help? I can assign more crew to you if you need it."

"No. no. My staff is getting everything under control. We have wounded that need a real hospital with rejuvenation tanks and med-tables. How soon until we can transport to a major facility?"

"Soon, Doc. Its priority one for us." He motions to the makeshift medical hut. "You'll have to work with what you've got a little while longer."

He pats Tilley on the back and turns back to Connor to continue their tour. "Make sure Doc Tilley has everything he needs, Connor. Strip everything we have down to the frame if you have to. Our wounded must come first. Understood?"

"Yes sir. I have Shurtz working with a support detail to do just that."

"Well done, Lieutenant. Do you have a final count now?"

"Yes sir. Nineteen convoy vessels were able to get off pods or emergency vehicles before being boarded. We have nine hundred and eleven convoy crewmen and two hundred forty-nine Strantos survivors."

"Do we know how many crew were on the convoy when it was taken?"

"We have a rough guess, sir. Lieutenant Shurtz interviewed what we left of the convoy bridge personnel and crew. Approximately five hundred and thirty crew were taken."

J'Kal feels a rage rising from her gut, threatening to overcome her Talusha training. Her finger nails dig deep grooves into the side of the hospital door panel.

"This is monstrous! Those cowards have never caused so much damage or casualties. Just for some lousy supplies. Why now? Why this convoy?" Her voice swiftly rises in a crescendo of pure hate. "We need to find these bastards and skin them alive. Slowly."

There is a stunned silence around her. On the bridge, Eva commands with a stern calmness, never out of control. She glances around and turns several shades of reds.

She straightens and forces her body to relax so she can compose herself. "I'm sorry, Captain. That was uncalled for."

Captain Sprague shakes his head and says, "No apologies needed, Eva. You're just venting what we are all feeling. Outrage and loss. We will not let this stand. I give you my word." He looks around at the small crowd surrounding them, most with bowed heads, still stunned from the battle. "Understand this, everyone. We will find the animals that did this and bring them to justice!"

He turns to Connor and draws him close. "Have you made contact with anyone in Tanadoc?"

"Yes sir. They are sending medical help and transports to take us back to Tanadoc. They have mostly farming land transports and not many of those. They're sending everything they have. It will be two days before they arrive, best case. Travel on this moon is very difficult with the mountainous terrain. I'll keep tabs on their progress."

He nods to the left at the small shack being assembled just to their left. "We've just set up a temporary base of operations and have it staffed with Marines and whatever security forces we have from the convoy."

Sprague surveys the scene, more than satisfied with the effort. "Well done, Mr. Connor." He motions for Connor stand in front of him and for J'Kal to stand by his side. "Stand at attention please." Lieutenant Connor covers his confusion quickly. Sprague removes a pip from his own collar and pins it on Connors then raises his hand in salute. "Unfortunately for you, you've just been field promoted to Lieutenant in charge of Strantos Base."

Lieutenant Connor returns his salute, unable to hide a smile.

"As you were, Lieutenant. Take Mr. Shurtz in hand and coordinate with the remaining bridge officers. We need to get these people settled until we can transport them to Tanadoc. And get me an accurate status of personnel and equipment as soon as possible."

Connor exchanges a crisp salute and turns on a heel. He waves to an officer helping to stack crates of supplies next to the door of the shack. "Mr. Shurtz, gather all bridge officers at the med tent in five." He brings the comtat on his arm to life, the embedded crimson circuit lines glowing just under the skin. He starts making notes as he strides towards the tent.

"That poor man, Captain. He has no idea what just happened. One moment he was an able bodied, competent bridge officer and now he's about to find out what being responsible for a thousand civilian and naval crewmen means. I hope he knows how to herd cats." Eva's smirk is genuine. "He'll be cursing you in a few days, you know."

"Yes. He will either run screaming from the promotion soon or be transformed into a topnotch officer. My money is on the latter." It was Sprague's turn to smirk. "I personally researched and interviewed every officer I brought onboard Strantos, Eva, including you. Connor and Shurtz have real potential. Let's hope Connor lives up to it, fast."

Chapter Seven

OK. I can't feel my body. I can't see a thing. Wherever I am, it's as cold as an Eskimo's toes. Oh God, I'm breathing some thick, fizzing, liquid snot. How the hell is that possible? It fills my lungs and throat. I've had three day Mad Dog Twenty-Twenty binge hang overs that were better than this.

Finally, Pixie's voice resonates in the goo surrounding me. "Stand by, Jake. The genetic manipulation is complete. We're beginning the post op rinse and drain. As soon as you can, cough hard a few times to clear your lungs."

"OK. But..." Aaahhhhhhhhhh!

Iceberg cold spray hits my body, snapping my eyes open wide and sending me into convolutions from head to, to, uh, "WHAT are THOSE? Aaaaaahhhhhhhhh! My feet! They're wrinkly, pink alligator claws! What the hell?"

Nanel is outside the tank, peering in at my naked body. "Calm down, Jake. You knew what the bio-morph was going to do. We showed you the model. Cowboy up and get a grip on your... uh, self." She's got a wicked leer and is pointing a finger at my face. "Hold still and let the system drain the bio-mass. You're such a wuss!"

The chilling spray stops and a light tornado of hot air circulates around me, quickly vaporizing the remaining goo. When the swirling cloud dissipates, the clear tank cylinder recedes into the deck, leaving me standing in all my newly transformed awesomeness. Pixie warned me that my DNA changes are a mixture of animals throughout the Galaxies. Just call me the Cosmic Mutt. Gathering my inner strength, I turn to the console to get a first look of me in its reflection.

"Holy Crap!" There is no way prepare for this, no matter how much you play with the models. My fanged, drooling jaw hangs wide open showing multiple rows of razor edged teeth that point back towards my throat. Four, six inch fangs, two above and two below, protrude outward slightly. I resist the temptation to close my jaws just yet. I flick out my tongue. It's forked, black and long enough to lick my eyes if I wanted to. How the hell am I supposed to keep my teeth from slicing the thing off?

I must be seven feet tall, even sitting on my massive haunches. I try to stand and immediately start to fall over, unable to get my balance. I reach out to the closest console to steady myself and send a talon deep into the metal surface, sending sparks flying. Oops! I squat back down, fighting to get my equilibrium back.

Nanel puts a steadying hand on a bulging shoulder. "Easy Jake, it will take a little time to learn how to control your new body. Don't make any sudden moves for a while. We'll use this room to rehabilitate you and Arlo, once we run some tests. For starters you should fold your teeth back into their sockets until you need them."

I concentrate on my teeth, all bazillion of them, and try to move them back. Nuts. In the reflection I can see about half of them folding back. It looks like I'm an old fighter with dozens of teeth knocked out. Oh well. I concentrate and try again. All the extended teeth slowly retract into their slots. Better. Though I'm not sure it matters. A shark with its teeth retracted still looks like a shark and is just as dangerous.

I break my glaze from the monster in the mirror. "Hey, where's Arlo?" I whip my head around and almost smack Pixie in the head. Good thing she's short.

"Watch it, Jake, that's your girlfriend's head you almost took off!" She slaps my pink thigh and points to the side. "Your partner is finishing his rinse cycle now. Take a look."

The other tank in the room is retracting into the floor, small bits of goo and mucus spattering the floor. In the center of the mess my buddy Arlo is 'standing' on his back four legs and waving his 'arms' around in front of his face.

My 'little' partner is now almost five feet long, tail tip to snout. His skin reminds me of all the scaled dragon skins from my favorite fantasy stories. Each small scale is gleaming, pearlescent black with a bloody red tip. His triangular, horn tipped head looks totally bad ass cool. His neck spikes are bright yellow with blue tips. He stretches his jaw and a forked, red snaky tongue shoots out and back.

Arlo turns to me and croaks, "Tude! Dis is owzum! Wai! Tid Ah ust zeak?" He snaps his head to Nanel, his eyes pivoting forward. "Pease zell me dis will get getr!"

Everyone in the room cracks up, me included. Arlo turns a bright red from stem to stern with a dozen blotches of icky green pulsing over his body. "Hey buddy! Great to see you still have your skin cammo tricks! You're either embarrassed or pissed as hell! Tell me it's the first, I hope you haven't lost your snarky sense of humor!"

Arlo's scaly skin slowly stops pulsing, the color fading to a deep maroon. Dim rings of black flow, one after the other, slowly down the full length of his body.

"Rerax, Cake, seeing you goust caught me oftcard." He rotates his eyes back to Nanel. "Seens ike Ahm geddin bedder already."

Nanel nods her head, pleased with the way Arlo and Jake have made it through the bio-morph so far. "Yes, Arlo. You seem to be adjusting quickly. The more you speak the faster you'll adapt.

Could you please try your telepathic link? I want to verify it's still strong."

A booming cackle echoes in my brain, making me cringe. "I sure hope so! 10-4, good buddies, y'all got your ears on?"

"Ow, Arlo, turn down the volume, will you?"

I catch myself reflexively trying to cover my ears just in time. Another inch and I would have performed the first self-lobotomy. Nanel and Pixie press their hands over their ears, obviously overwhelmed by Arlo's telepathic power as well.

"Uh, sorry, mate. Is this better?" His voice is almost normal now. Not painful, but it's still too loud.

"Down another notch, man."

His voice is pretty normal this time. "OK, OK. How's this, guys?"

Nanel and Pixie nod their heads as they lower their hands. Pixie says, "Much better, Arlo. It's pretty obvious that your telepathy has been greatly enhanced. Without your implants, this could be a great help to your mission."

"I yust hope I cin top soundin lik ah frog wid a mouth fula arbles soon," Arlo says, his jaw grinding up and down, left and right. It's got to be as painful as it looks.

"You're doing great, buddy. Just keep trying."

"Indeed, gentlemen. You both need to stretch your abilities, learn your new body quickly. We only have a little time to get you ready for insertion. We hope to get you into place before the next raids occurs. Our Intel is sketchy but we think we have less than two weeks to prepare." Nanel is dead serious again. She turns to Pixie and says, "Lieutenant, I leave them in your charge. Ship has prepared a rigorous rehabilitation regimen. You will all stay in this lab, working through that routine until you are confident that Arlo and Jake are capable of infiltrating the mercenaries without being discovered."

To Arlo and me she says, "You two continue to show amazing valor and bravery. You are taking an incredible risk. Again. The Galaxies have no way to repay you for all your sacrifices." She leans in and kisses Arlo on his scaly snout. Then she moves to me, takes my clawed hand, reaching up to give me a short, warm kiss on my bunny lips. She turns and starts toward the exit. Over her shoulder she says, "I'll check with you over a secure channel, Tillet. No one is to enter or exit this room until we're ready. Keep them sweating and report any problems immediately." She steps through the wall without another word.

It takes me a few seconds to recover from Nanel's kiss. It's sort of like downing a three olive, pepper martini in one gulp. My rubbery lips are still tingling and warm. I look over and Arlo is trying to whistle, both eyes scanning the ceiling. "You might want to pay attention to your sweetie pie, numb nuts," he prods me in my mind. His eyes slowing rotate down where Pixie is standing in front me, her arms crossed and one eyebrow raised. *Oops*.

Her voice would curdle fresh milk. "So, Mr. Jasper. One kiss by an Adrian and you forget all about your 'Pixie'? Should I move my things out while you're gone?"

Crap! "Not fair, not fair. She surprised me, you saw it! Arlo, you saw it too, right. Tell her."

Arlo's laugh sounds more like a gurgling toilet bowl. "You on ur own, Cake."

It's hard to balance on my huge butt, wave my pink paws in front of me and look contrite, but I try anyway. "No, Pixie, please. She just caught me off guard, that's all. You know I love you. I'd never…"

Pixie's beautiful face almost exploded with laughter. She drops her arms and doubles over. "Relax, lover. I couldn't resist." She climbs up my torso and grabs my head in both of her tiny hands. She plants a wet, rubbery kiss on my wet, rubbery lips. Her eyes are sparkling like two polished tanzanite gems. I can lose myself in those amazing eyes. "Would I kiss that face if I didn't love you, silly boy?"

She climbs back down, careful to avoid my claws. She moves back to the far side of the lab and says, "OK. Enough play, let's get serious." Her fingers play across the console and a large treadmill with side bars rises from the floor. "Jake, it's time to learn how to walk. Careful, if you break this equipment it's coming out of your pay."

She glances at Arlo, her arms back on her hips. "And you, Arlo. You're going to need to get control of an extra pair of limbs and learn to talk quickly." She presses more control pads and another treadmill rises. "Since you don't have your implants any more I want you two to start talking out loud while you're training. You'll need a solid, coherent plan if you're going to fool the mercenaries and join the crew of one of their vessels."

I hobble over to my treadmill, wobbling like crazy, trying to stay upright. Before I can settle in, the belt starts to move, almost toppling me backwards. "Hey, PIP, easy! If I fall I may not be able to get up!" The machine stops abruptly.

PIP responds over the lab intercom. "My apologies, Mr. Jasper, but Lieutenant Commander Nanel has instructed me to push you hard. Shall we begin, sir?"

Before I can protest, the treadmill starts moving again and I have to scramble to stay upright. Arlo's machine is moving too, and he's having a hard time coordinating with his extra limbs. He bangs his snout on the front bar and swears, "Damn!"

"Hey, your first coherent word, little buddy! Well done." I can't help taking a jab at Arlo. His spikey face is crimson red and there is a violent yellow ring flowing down his skin. His eyes laser me. If looks could vaporize, I'd be space dust.

Arlo speaks again, "Hey PIP, it loochs like Cake is doin musch better, maybe he needs mora speed."

My machine revs up a notch, my oversized bunny legs failing a bit until I get them under control.

"OK. OK. Easy on the speed, PIP. You do not want these claws to take out a console or two. Take it back down a bit until I get my stride under control, please." The treadmill slows a bit.

Pixie steps between the exercise machine and motions to both of us. "You two need to push yourselves. Concentrate on controlling your new bodies." She looks at the small vid display on her arm comtat and says, "Ship's first workout has you doing ninety minutes on the treads, upping the speed one notch every five minutes. You'll need to really focus, gentlemen."

She motions to Arlo, "Your vocal training starts now as well." She glances at the nearest console screen which is slowly scrolling text from top to bottom. "Vocalize each word as it scrolls down. Ship has created an increasingly difficult word and phrase lesson for you. The harder you try the fastest you'll adapt."

Arlo nods his head and says, "Es, mam." He glances back at the screen and moans. Then he starts reading out loud. "Cee thpot. See spoth run." Arlo glances over to me and mentally says, "If you say a word, bag o' bones, I'll rip your tongue out and sew it to your nose!" He turns back to the screen. "Ron, spot, run."

Before I can give him a good jib my treadmill speeds up a notch and PIP says, "Mr. Jasper will not have the time or energy to ridicule your lessons, Arlo. I intend to keep you both very busy."

Pixie smirks and turns to her console. "Very good, Ship. I'll monitor our charges as well. If I need to motivate them I know where I can find a cattle prod." She gives me a wicked wink and says, "Not that I think I'll need it here."

Great. Huge pink body. Uncooperative muscles. Dangerous claws instead of hands. And a pretty girlfriend I can't kiss anymore. This is going to be big time fun.

Nuts!

Chapter Eight

Deep in the bowels of Sewer City, nestled near the power core where few people have business, is the cramped sanctuary of Captain Ryan G'radian and Bolton. Bolton is the last surviving member of G'radian's family after a misguided raid by the FTG. The FTG cruiser 'Eleusis' attacked G'radian's compound after being tipped that the compound harbored GHA raiders ready to attack an FTG outpost. But G'radian's home was home only to honest traders.

The FTG tried to apologize and compensate the compound for the raid. For Ryan G'radian the reparation was hollow and cold. He wanted desperately to seek revenge. His heart said an eye for an eye. But the code of honor for his clan forbids it. So he swore on his family's graves that he would find the bridge officers of the Eleusis and sell them all into slavery, a fate Ryan felt was appropriate.

Captain G'radian had found all but two of the officers he blamed for the raid; the Captain and a junior Officer. The Captain was Alex Groff. The junior officer is now the Captain of the Triumph, Selenia Sol'anotta Starla.

The FTG made an example of the Captain. Groff was court martialed and dishonorably discharged. He vanished immediately and has not been seen since. G'radian continues his search for Groff, eager to cast his vengeance upon the stupid bastard.

Because Starla was a newly billeted junior officer, G'radian has different plans for her. He knows she is not going underground like the coward Groff. He is taking his time, looking for the right time to impose his revenge upon her. And impose it he will.

G'radian is staring into his mug of the local brew at Gray's bar. It's a tiny, hole in the wall favorite of those who want to remain unnoticed on Sewer City. More of a narrow niche in the hall, barely large enough to hold a dozen patrons. G'radian is in his usual stall, sitting across from Bolton.

"Are you going to drink that or stare it to death, Father?" Bolton's lopsided smirk shows off his handsome, tattooed face. "I'd ask what you're thinking about, but it's either Mother or how to finish your vendetta. I prefer to think it's the first." Bolton raises his mug and takes a cold, burning swig.

G'radian doesn't respond. He just keeps swirling his mug, his eyes smoldering, his lips tight and thin.

"Father." Bolton speaks softly, trying to get through his father's dark mood. Lightly tapping his mug on the metal tabletop, he raises his voice slightly. "Father. You've got to get past this hate. It's like a burning cancer inside of you. It's all you think about. It controls you like…"

G'radian slams his own mug on the table, the drink spilling over the edges, the sound unnaturally load in this small space. "Enough!" He looks around, thankful that there are no other patrons to hear his outburst. He looks over his shoulder at Dar, the pudgy barkeeper. Dar is glaring at him, his blaster on the bar, waiting to see if he'll need it.

"I'm sorry, Dar. You won't need that pea shooter, I promise. You couldn't hit a thagg at ten pace with that thing anyway."

Dar sniffs at the insult, but slips the blaster back under the counter. "Maybe you find out someday, you maybe do I think." He turns back and starts pushing the grime on the counter top around, one of his ten stalked eyes fixed on G'radian.

"Father…" starts Bolton.

"No, son, stop." G'radian leans back, the metal chair groaning. "I know you don't approve of my mission. That doesn't matter, I'm going to pursue the last of the murderers and give them the fate they deserve." He eyes his son, saddened at the distance this is putting between them. "Until Starla and Groff have slave collars around their disgusting necks, my family won't sleep in final peace." He leans forward again, grabbing the mug and taking a long swig.

It's Bolton's turn to slam his mug on the table. This time Dar dives under the bar, surprised by the young man's outburst. He decides to stay low, to hell with the bar.

"Now YOU stop, Father!" He slings the mug against the near wall, shattering it. "Do NOT justify this madness on the souls of our family. Mother would never want this, you know this is true. Only the lunacy of your grief keeps you from seeing the truth." He rises, backing away from the table. "How much longer will you allow this sickness to consume you? You are no longer the father I knew as a boy."

He turns to walk away, his head dipping sadly. "You know I will never leave you. I love you deeply. But I miss the man who was my father."

Bolton strides from the bar and turns down the hall. G'radian watches the boy, no, the man, who is his only close companion, his only family, walk away. His only son. When did he grow so tall? When did he start walking in the boots of a trader?

G'radian swirls his mug again, thinking on the Bolton's words. In his heart he wonders if his son is right. Is he wasting precious years trying to revenge his family? He unconsciously reaches for the simple band of gold on his hand, turning it slowly on his finger. He can almost feel the worn inscription against his skin. *'Forever, my Love'*.

A red hot heat returns to his heart. They took you from me in an instant. They will pay for it for all eternity.

He stands and throws a credit on the table. "There, Dar, this should pay for the mess and the drinks. You can come out now." He strides from the bar, intent again on how to exact his pound of flesh.

*****

The dim, dank corridor at the center of Sewer City hums with the soft swooshing sound of ventilation and machinery buried deep behind the walls, floors and ceiling. Bolton is accustomed to the vibrations beneath his feet and constant pings from the metal walls. His boots click softly as he strides back to their small hideaway.

His heart is heavy after failing, again, to turn his father's mind away from this course of madness. He strokes the bony ridges of his chin and mutters to the hollow walls, "How do I make you realize that Mother and Gran and Sis and all of our friends cannot rest until you let them? The revenge you seek only feeds your hate and anger. It has taken control of you and I don't know how to break that hold."

He peers cautiously around the last corner, looking for possible threats. Seeing none, he presses the rusting rivet in the wall that turns off the security system long enough for him to slide the wall panel aside and step through to the room. The panel slides back silently, a small red indicator above the door signals that the system has been reengaged.

The comm station is beeping insistently. Bolton hesitates, he usually lets his father handle incoming messages. He decides it's time he took more responsibility for their operation even if some of it he despises. He palms the system and says, "Identify yourself." He waits for the response, suspecting it is one of their mercenary ship captains. He was right.

"I am Cauldun Rayt, youngling. I would speak to Captain G'radian. Where can I find him?" The gravelly voice of the Grockna mercenary is loud and haughty. "Run along and fetch him for me, boy. I have returned with much booty and I want what the Captain promised me."

Bolton bristles at the slight, but knows better than to confront the fool before his father can speak to him. "Ten minutes in the usual place, Rayt. Bring your manners with you this time."

Before Cauldun can retort he slaps the switch off and taps his wrist communicator. Captain G'radian answers immediately. "What is it?"

"Cauldun Rayt has returned. He claims he's made a big strike. I've sent him to the meeting point. I'm leaving now to meet him."

"Stay sharp, son. Cauldun has turned out to be just another mindless thug. He has no honor. He's one of my worst mistakes. I'm going to cut him loose today and he won't be happy about it."

Bolton's comm link goes dead. He grabs his mini-blaster and slips it into his left boot. Then he straps on his blaster holster and ties it tight. He is glad they are severing ties with Rayt, he never liked the man's attitude. Father should have done a better job checking the mercenary's reputation before bringing him in. He turned out to be vicious, greedy and unpredictable.

Bolton slips through the panel and heads down the corridor, eager to get this meeting over with.

After two minutes of zagging through the maze of passages he suddenly steps to his right, slipping into a dark crack in the wall, still a few meters short of the rendezvous chamber. He knows Rayt will have to take this path and he wants to be behind him before entering the room, just in case there is trouble. Bolton is sure that his father will already be inside, waiting for the mercenary.

Seconds later he hears loud footsteps of three men on the metal floor coming around the corner. Rayt isn't bothering to hide his approach, as arrogant as always. Expecting to see them pass him he listens for the panel to slide. Instead the footsteps have stopped just outside his hiding place.

Cauldun Rayt's voice is low but Bolton can hear his growl echoing off the metal walls of the corridor. His blood runs cold as he hears Rayt say, "Remember you two tarl-heads, wait until he's turned over the credits, then you take out the youngling and I'll take out G'radian. I'm going to snap his arrogant neck and then we'll take over their operation."

Bolton is shaking with fury, barely able to keep his anger is check. Even with the element of surprise he won't get all three before they kill him. Then his father will be next. He taps his communicator three times, hoping his father will notice and know something is up.

Cauldun slams a huge fist on the panel twice, eager to get his credits and take over G'radian's operations. "Open up, Captain. I'm here to get my due." A wicked smile cracks his face as the panel starts to open. He whispers under his breath, "And time you get yours."

Chapter Nine

"Lieutenant Connor, report." Sprague and J'Kal are making their final inspection of the makeshift base camp before the suns go down. Sprague taps his arm comtat again, the spidery filaments pulsing at his wrist. "Lieutenant Connor, report please." Sprague's implant was somehow damaged in the battle. Sprague will need a full med lab to find and fix the problem. In the meantime the comtat will have to do.

Connor's tinny voice emanates from a tiny bionic speaker embedded with the comtat. "Connor here, sir. Communication is still spotty as you can tell. Many of the crew have damaged implants and comtats. We believe there was some kind of EMP event, probably a weapon of some kind used by the mercenaries just as we completed the transit."

"Understood, Connor. What about the base and the crew status?"

"Strantos Base is secure, sir. Doc Tilley has attended to all the critically wounded and has set up recovery rooms in the 'Atlas' and the 'Dominot' shuttle craft. He believes all the current wounded will survive, but has requested, again, immediate evac to a med lab for ten critical patients."

"Have you had contact with Tannadoc?"

"Yes sir. They are doing everything they can to get here quickly with a portable med lab. Supplies and base support will be close behind." Connor's voice sputters a bit and then he continues. "The crew count hasn't changed from our initial report. The only thing we still cannot determine is exactly how many civilians were on board all vessels. Some records did not survive so we won't know until we can contact Fleet Headquarters."

"Very well. Keep me informed on the status of the Tannadoc convoy. Do whatever you can to prepare for their arrival so we get the wounded immediate medical attention."

"Yes sir." Sprague's link goes silent. He and Eva have stopped in front of a makeshift kitchen. Crewmen and civilians are pitching in together, setting up shuttle and pod hull panels as improvised tables and setting out rations.

Lieutenant Shurtz has his sleeves rolled up, his uniform soiled with dried blood and grime. He's finishing another table and directing a young Spritezoid woman with the setup of the food. Her bright blue spiked hair and neon blue eyes are typical of the S'pritia inhabitants. Or were, rather, as theirs was one of the first planets aquaformed by the GHA.

"Alana, let's get these rations on the table so we can start feeding the civilians. We've got enough tables set up to start serving now." Shurtz stands back and stretches his back and rubs his shoulders. Surprised by the sudden appearance of the Captain, he straightens up and salutes sharply.

"Sorry, sir, I didn't see you coming."

"As you were, Mr. Shurtz, we just finished checking on the compound. I was hoping you had the chow ready. I know we have a lot of hungry people who need to eat and get some rest." Sprague looks around, pleased with the way his people are stepping up to their tasks. "You've done a great job, Mister."

He pauses next to the petite Spritezoid, putting out a hand in thanks. "Alana, is it?"

Alana wipes her hand on her apron and gives Sprague a firm handshake and a warm smile.

"Yes, Captain. Alana Novega."

"I can't tell you how much I appreciate the help that you and others have given. It helps to keep everyone busy and feeling needed. We need to keep everyone's spirits up and show that we're doing everything possible."

A weary smile spreads across Alana's face and she tilts her head to the side. "It's the least we can do, Captain. We all know that without the bravery and sacrifice of your crew we all would have either perished or been sold into slavery. We thank you."

She rises on her tiptoes and lightly kisses him on the cheek, leaving a dark red lipstick smudge. "My people show our appreciation openly. I hope it doesn't offend you." She steps back, hands behind her back. "You'll have to excuse me, Captain, I see we have hungry mouths to feed here." She turns back to the tables and begins welcoming and serving. Mr. Shurtz salutes and hurries to assist her.

Eva nudges the Captain gently. "You're blushing, sir. Does that mean you were offended by that 'appreciation'?" She smiles it his obvious discomfort. "Relax, sir. I'd kiss you myself, but, well, military protocol and all that." She reaches up and rubs the red smudge from his cheek. "There, no one will know you're adored by a pretty little Spritezoid."

Sprague brushes his cheek, not unpleased with the show of affection. It occurs rarely because of his position. Straightening up and brushing his tunic, he says, "Thank you, Eva."

He gazes at his XO, appreciating her anew. Military life does limit emotional attachments. No one knows when they'll be suddenly separated or worse. His XO has always been there to support and guide him. Now he can see what his hectic life has glazed over.

He takes Eva's hand, looking into those intelligent eyes. "You have always been more than an XO to me, Eva, I hope you know that. Your support and companionship has helped me through more trials than I can remember. This ordeal has shown me that I need to be more open with my feelings. I hope we can continue this conversation soon."

He releases her hand and steps back. "But for now, we need to complete our inspection. Are you with me, XO?"

Eva's eyes are misty and bright. She's wanted to share her feelings for the Captain for some time now. Like the Captain, her job has always overridden any chance of voicing those feelings.

She grabs Sprague's collar and pulls him in for a light, heady kiss. When she steps back she says, "I've wanted to do that for years, John Sprague. Yes. We will talk more. Soon." She smiles and exhales. "After you, sir." She gestures to the right, matching his stride.

Chapter Ten

"OK, Arlo, I've had enough of this rehab crap. How about you?" I've just dropped my thousand pound barbells on the floor with a loud clunk. Arlo has his three-D goggles on, prancing around in some simulated Jedi sword battle. It's his favorite past time. Yea. Silly looking he is.

It's been almost two weeks since our bio-morph. PIP has been pushing us eighteen hours a day with coordination training. It's been a bitch getting used to my massive pink bunny body. Even figuring out how to eat with these huge shark teeth and fangs has been a challenge. My body metabolism forces me to eat raw meat washed down with gallons of beer. Unfortunately the beer metabolizes so fast I don't even get a buzz from it.

Arlo has fared much better than me. He adapted to his extra limbs and larger size quickly. His problems have been utilizing his 'arms', something totally foreign to him. The immersion simulator is just the thing to help him develop some ninja skills. His new vocal chords have settled down as well. I swear he's even mastered a decent Sean Connery voice. It's got a little Peewee Herman mixed in but otherwise it's pretty good.

Arlo takes off his goggles, tossing them on the console. "I was just thinking the same thing, Bunny Boy. Enough practice, let's get this show on the road."

Arlo drops his simulator wand next to the googles and says, "Ship. When are we gonna get this mission started? We want to kick some mercenary boo-tah and get back to our handsome selves!"

"I have reported your progress to Captain Starla. I believe you are both as ready physically as you can be. I suggest that you finalize your background story so that it's second nature to you. You need to be convincing mentally as well as physically."

Lieutenant Tillet enters through the portal and walks towards Arlo. "Ship is right. We need to make sure your cover is rock solid. If those mercenaries think you two are FTG plants, you can kiss your partner's pink ass goodbye." She gives me a wicked wink, "And I would be very upset if that boo-tah did not come back to me."

Arlo actually looks hurt and puts a hand over his chest. His voice is low and sexy. "Lieutenant. Surely you meant to say that you'd miss my charismatic charm and witty repartee. Jake's wrinkly behind can't be that attractive."

"Hey. I'm right here. And my behind is NOT wrinkly, it has character."

Pixie chuckles, probably aware that all this gee-gawing is just a cover for how frickin' terrified Arlo and I are.

She gets that 'I'm serious' look and leans back on one of the consoles. "OK. Enough joking. Captain Starla, Ship and I agree that it's time to insert you into one of the outlaw crews. It's time to give Jake his collar and go over your cover one last time. You'll be leaving for a rendezvous tomorrow at oh eight hundred."

Crap! Tomorrow? Well. Always be careful what you ask for. "How are we going to get to Sewer City?"

Captain Starla strides into the lab, a small suitcase in hand. "The Lieutenant will be transporting you on a freighter that has been added to Sewer City's delivery schedule to arrive tomorrow. Once you have debarked and the freighter's cargo has been unloaded she will depart immediately. We don't want to draw attention."

She sets the case on a console, pops it open and draws out a dull black collar. It looks more like a thick rubber band, about two inches high. Several rows of tiny red lights circle around the collar.

"This collar will adapt to your neck so you can move. It's a real slave collar, Jake, we can't take any chances on a fake." She hands Arlo another dull black device. "This is your controller, Arlo. Again, it's real."

Tillet takes the collar and says, "Bend over Jake, it's time to become a slave. Arlo, open the collar with the remote."

I bend low. I have to be careful not to squash my girlfriend. Arlo puts the controller on his wrist and presses a stud. The collar separates along an almost invisible seam. Tillet slings the end of the collar around my neck, grabbing the end. She brings the ends together and suddenly they snap together again.

She nods to Arlo. My partner presses another stud. I can feel the collar lock and flow around my neck. It's snug but not tight. No way I could get it over my head, but I can breathe with no problem. A feeling of dread runs up my spine. "Guys. This is horrible. No being should feel this way. How can the FTG allow the slave market to exist?"

"We don't, Jake!" Starla says tersely. "We campaign every culture to abandon this disgusting practice. But we have to live within the local laws. Otherwise we would be just another dictatorship, forcing our version of right and wrong on the galaxy."

"But…"

"No buts, Jake. It takes time, but most cultures do stop the practice with our urging and a few well-placed sanctions on trade."

Pixie laughs nervously and says, "Of course another part of that is because the FTG has saved their asses from, or serves as a deterrent against, the GHA. Regardless of the reasons, they seem to have a change of heart when we tell them the practice may prevent them from entering into the Galactic Union's trade guilds."

"It's amazing how trade will motivate cultural change, isn't it." Pixie has hands on her hips, voice dripping with sarcasm. "But the Captain is right. It takes time and leverage to make those in power change their social and economic mores. Almost every culture we've met has or did have slavery in some form at one point in their history. Not everyone can be made to see the error though."

Arlo cocks his head to side and nods. "OK. OK. History lesson is over. Where do we go from here? Bun-zilla and me want to stop the bad guys and get our own adorable bodies back as soon as possible."

Starla nods back and says, "Right. What cover story have you worked out?"

Tapping my collar uncomfortably, I give her a condensed version we've come up with. "Arlo won me in a winner take all gambling game. Now he takes me around the gladiator circuit to fight for money. We heard about the mercenary gig at one of the fights. Arlo was a first mate on a few pirate ships in the Arctos sector. It's a distant quadrant that no one is likely to know."

Arlo jumps in. "I want a chance to strike it rich on one the supply ambushes. I'll sign on as a Chief Mate or Skipper if I can. Jake will be my 'muscle'. Since you ripped our implants out, we'll have a find another way to contact you, hopefully before the ambush."

Pixie's face is full of concern. "Jake, all of this will be a waste if you can't tell us in advance. We'll need to know which ship you board and when and where the attack will be. Without all that information we won't be able to get to the right delivery point in time to stop the ambush and capture the mercenaries. And we need to send a clear message to anyone else contemplating ambushing our ships."

"The Lieutenant is correct, Mr. Jasper. Headquarters sends out over a hundred supply missions a week. We scramble the missions so that it's harder to track them, especially since the ambushes have escalated," says the Captain fretfully. "We know there is a mole somewhere in headquarters, but so far we haven't been able to find it. Discover who that cowardly bastard is and I'll guarantee you a front row seat when I stretch his or her neck."

I see the problem, but not the answer so much. "If we can get a message to you in time how are you going to be able stop the ambush? No matter how many ships you have in standby, you probably won't be able to get there before the supply convoy. It will all be over in those first few minutes and the mercs will be gone."

Pixie shakes a negative. "That's not the plan, Mr. Jasper. If you to feed us your ship and target convoy information we can fold just before the convoy and take out any mercenaries before you arrive. No one knows about you or our plan so far, so the chances are good that the mole won't be able to tip them off." She raises a hand and continues, "That's the ideal outcome, but in the least you'll have info on one or more the merc leaders, like G'radian."

Arlo snorts out loud and croaks, "There are a lot of holes in this plan, Lieutenant, but Jake and I are still ready to go. It's time to put a stop to this."

Captain Starla rises from the console and steps to stand in front of Arlo and me. I can see the concern on her face.

"We're all hoping you'll be able to complete this mission and come home to us, gentlemen. Once again you two are going well above and beyond. I don't want you to take unnecessary chances with your lives." She smiles, the look of concern gone. "Of course if the past is any indication, you'll do whatever you want anyway."

I give the Captain a bunny salute. "Our motto, sir, is 'It's better to apologize for a screw up than to ask permission to screw up.'" I drop my pink arm with a snap, digging a claw into my thigh. "Damn! Next time I want to be a Grockna, not 'Hare Scissor-Hands'."

Chapter Eleven

"This is a freighter? Pixie, you've got to be kidding me, this POS won't make it out of the hanger deck, much less the transit to Sewer City!"

The 'Hyperion' is an ancient cargo freighter that looks like Noah used it to ferry the hippos to the ark. It's a huge, squat, grey bug, crouching off kilter on three good and one broken landing struts. Some of the side panels are dirty red, obviously not original equipment. The forward windshield looks like it was taken from a couple of old Peterbilt tractors and glued together. There is rust everywhere, probably the only thing holding the pieces of this heap together.

Arlo shakes his head and mutters, "This is the best the FTG could do?"

Tillet slaps Arlo on a leg. "Stop whining, Arlo. I'll have you know the 'Hyperion' is a great ship. I've been working on her while you two were goldbricking. It's not easy making a ship look this pathetic, trust me."

"Well, you did a great job in that case. I've seen garbage scows that would put, uh, 'Hyperion' to shame. And about the name. 'Hyperion'? Wasn't that one of the Titans of Earth mythology? Hmmm, kinky. If I remember my Greek mythology right he and his sister were an item. Weren't their kids the Sun, the Moon and…"

Pixie hand is in that 'you stop right there' position every woman has mastered. "OK. OK. Get your mind back on point, mister, not everything is about sex!" She drops her hand and winks at me. "Well, not right now anyway."

I love my girlfriend.

Pixie has shed her stark white FTG uniform for a worn and scruffy trader's outfit, complete with dirty black combat boots, low slung blaster holster and black beret tilted to one side of her head. Her stained white shirt is sleeveless, a combat jacket fitted loosely over it.

I still have my reservations about this 'great' ship. "Can we at least slap a coat of paint on it to hide the rust?"

"No. This is the best camouflage we could have for the mission. No one will pay any attention to this ship. I should be able to slip into the docking area, unload and slip out without anyone other than the Cargo Master taking notice of us. You'll be my cargo crew. You'll unload and then slip off somewhere inside the cargo bay."

Arlo says, "Yeah. Our intel says there are lots of drinking establishments around the docking area. Go figure. Hopefully we can find where the mercs are hiring quickly. The longer we stay there, the hinkier it looks."

Pixies raises an eyebrow. "It's our hope too, but you'll just have to improvise. Arlo has enough credits to keep you comfortable for a few weeks. If you haven't found a ship by then, you may as well contact us for pickup. We'll have to try another contact point."

I shake my head and interrupt. "Not a chance, Lieutenant! We're going to make contact on Sewer City, I promise you. We may not get another chance at this. We have to stop this now, before more people are hurt. We'll find a way. Right, Arlo?"

Arlo gives me the stinky eye, which is really creepy coming from his gyrating eyes. His Connery voice is getting damn good. "That's right, Ma'am. Pinky and I won't let you down. Shall we get moving? I'll go check out this hunk of junk. I'll try not to break anything."

Arlo adjusts the black leather straps that run across his chest, holding his vest harness in place. He's opted for this season's retro fashion in Pirate attire I see. Tiny pointy studs cover the vest and small gold chains adorns the back of the harness. He has a blaster holstered on each of the straps crisscrossing his chest. Not very haute couture, but effective. He raises up a little on his four legs and moves smoothly up the loading ramp and disappears into the cargo bay.

Pixie grabs my clawed hand and squeezes it tightly. "We may not have time on the trading post for goodbyes. I want to make sure you remember that you're mine even if you are a giant bunny rabbit." She stretches up and lightly kisses my fuzzy cheek. "You come back to me, Jake Jasper."

Warmth spreads though my wrinkly body like a sea breeze on Waikiki beach. I am such a lucky duffus. "I'd kiss you, baby, but I don't want to hurt you. I'll save the kiss for when Arlo and I get back."

Pixie smiles, wiping a tear from her eye. "You'd better, Jake, or I'll have to come kick your ass, wrinkles and all."

She heads up the ramp with me lumbering in close tow.

Jeez, we're really going to do this. How do I get myself into these messes?

Arlo slaps the ramp switch as Pixie and I step into the bay. The ramp complains with creaks, pops and low groans until it slams shut with a loud bang. It's so dim in here I can barely see Pixie and Arlo walking ahead of me towards the cockpit. It takes a few seconds before all the interior lights flicker on.

The bay is packed with crates of all sizes and shapes. Cargo boxes are the same across the Universe. Boxy. Mostly grey and scarred from being tossed and slammed around, well, packed cargo bays. Some have dazzling tariff stamps on them, others look like rock star tour cases with destinations on worlds I've never heard of. That's not that surprising, I guess. Arlo and I have only been with the FTG for a few years, most of it on the Triumph.

Pixie steps through the narrow hatch into the cockpit. She looks back at us in the bay, all steel and business now that we're doing this. "Strap in gentlemen, we launch in ten." Then she disappears to the right, snuggling into the captain's chair.

I grab the seat on the left side of the hatch so I can see into the cockpit. It's too small for a co-pilot or navigator so Pixie is going to be on her own. Every surface has a spinning dial, blinking light or flickering screen. Toggle switches are crammed between every device without any rhyme or reason that I can detect. Pixie went way out of her way to make this POS look old. Modern freighters basically have a 'Go' button on the console and a tiny little Atari joystick in the extreme case that the pilot has to take over flight.

A power surge dims the lights a little further as Pixie starts flipping switches and pushing buttons, bringing the ship to life. The low rolling whir suddenly breaks into a loud series of staccato thumping and banging under our feet. It sounds like a herd of hippos doing a flamenco dance in a room full of steel conga drums. Really. Just like it, I'm not kidding.

Pixie alternates cursing and slamming her fist on the console. "Damn!" Wham! "Damn!" Wham! "DAMN!" … There's a sharp ping from somewhere aft and suddenly the whir returns and then starts to swell. The hull starts to slowly oscillate up, down and all around, gently undulating like my old nuclear sub, the Bluefish, at flank bell. Wow, there's an ancient memory. Come to think of it, the more things change, the more they stay the same. Back then I traveled the depths of the seas in a metal tube. Today I'm plowing the stars in a metal box. Life is really weird. Just sayin'.

"Uh, Jake?" Arlo has taken the seat on the other side, strapping his lizardy body in as best he can. His beady eyes are kind of vibrating in small circles and his skin is turning a slimy, funky green. "Is the ship supposed to be bouncing like this? I don't think my new body has its sea legs yet." His eyes focus on the back corner of the bay, his lower jaw slowly pulsating. "I think I'm gonna heave breakfast into that hole over there."

Pixie spins around and shouts, "Don't you DARE upchuck in that bay, Mr. Arlo! This rig doesn't even have air conditioning, much less an air purifier. So just cowboy up and…"

"Bbbwwwwwaaaaaggggsstttt" A hot, steaming stream of liquid mucus and half-digested galactic insects arcs gracefully across bay into the far wall. "Spplllaaatttttt!" The dripping Pollock'esk puke-painting slides slowly down in the corner, making a disgusting multi-colored pool.

Arlo spits a bit of gnat leg to the side and I swear he look's sheepishly at me and then turns to the hatch. "Hmm. Sorry mates. Must have been those jalapeno crusted JunBa spiders I had for breakfast." He sniffs at the rising stench and gasps, "Yikes. You guys might want to hold your breath for the next few minutes, I'll see if I can find some Fabreze. Damn."

Pixie leans back into the bay and squeezes her eyes tightly shut. Her nose scrunches up. Her eyes pop open and she points a finger at Arlo and then me. "Damn you, Arlo! It's two hours to Sewer City, you moron. And we don't have time to ventilate, we have to leave now." She looks at the oozing artwork on the wall and says, "I don't care how you do it, but as soon as we've launched, you two will clean up that mess and get rid of the smell. DO. YOU. UNDERSTAND?!"

"Wait! What did I do? Arlo, hurled, not me. Why do I have to clean up his mess?"

The cockpit intercom chirps just in time to save the lightning bolts in Pixie's eyes from frying my tenders. "Hyperion, you are cleared to launch." There's a little chuckle and then. "Please be careful to not drop anymore parts on the way out, ok?"

Pixie snaps back, "Excuse me, crewman. Would you care to rephrase that last? Carefully."

"Uh, sorry, Hyperion. It won't happen again."

The poor crewman on launch duty has just realized his mistake. I hope Pixie forgets about this, or that dude is brig bound when she gets back.

"Lighten up a little, Pixie. This whole thing is making us all crazy. He didn't mean anything by it."

Pixie takes a big breath and holds it, turning towards me. Uh Oh. This could be exactly the wrong way to handle this. Again.

Her face loosens up a little and she lets the air out slowly. Her pretty nose is still scrunched up though.

"You're right, Jake. I'm wound up pretty tight right now." She glances at Arlo, who looks like he wants to retreat back into the womb. "But I mean it about the stench. As soon as we're clear, clean that mess up." She turns back to Arlo and says, "Are you OK, Arlo?"

Arlo nods his pale green head and leans back in the straps.

"Launch control, Hyperion. Launching now. Please excuse the mess on the deck."

I can hear the sigh of relief over the intercom. "Acknowledged, Hyperion. Sorry about the crack, Lieutenant. Be safe, Triumph wants you all returned in one piece."

Pixie nods to me. "Here we go, gentlemen. Button up tight, I think it's going to be a rough ride."

The bucket of bolts gives another low groan and then starts forward towards the launch bay shield. Pixie picks up some speed as we pass through the shield and accelerate 'down', across the Triumph's massive hull.

As we pass the bottom of the Nova Class Battleship, we veer away again and do a quick barrel row which almost cost me my own breakfast. That's what I get for looking out the viewport when Pixie is flying. Accelerating again, we quickly leave the Triumph behind.

"Time to see if this barge will fold, gentlemen. Hold on to your butts. Three. Two. One…"

"If? Wait a minute…"

Space stretches like a sheet of silly putty and does a flip around us. Arlo heaves and performs another acrobatic spew.

Great.

Chapter Twelve

Rayt's huge fist pounds on the door again. He nods to his men and they shift their weapons from their holsters to behind their backs.

Bolton's communicator vibrates twice, pauses and once again. His heart skips a beat but he stays in position. Rayt's pounding continues, his voice getting louder.

"Open up, G'radian. NOW! I want my credits!"

The panel slides open and Rayt starts to step through. Bolton quickly steps out of the shadows, his blaster held low but ready to use.

Rayt freezes before he can take a full step. His men are wide eyed and shocked still. Bolton quickly steps to the side of the panel where he can see them all, including his father.

G'radian's phasing-saber is crackling with angry green lightning barely an inch from Rayt's eyes. The blade seems almost alive, pulsing energy flowing slowly around the razor sharp edges. Small fingers of green and red energy dance from the tip of the sword along Rayt's brow. The merc's forehead is twitching with every tingle but he doesn't dare move.

"Your weapons. Drop them or Rayt will be missing the top of his head."

Rayt snarls and says, "My men will burn a hole in your friging head, you fool. We have you outnumbered."

Bolton puts his blaster in the earhole of the closest merc and says, "I believe the numbers are pretty even. My shot will take off this thug's head and burn a hole in thug number two there." Bolton pushes the nose of the blaster further into the ear of thug number one and snarls, "Weapons down. Now."

Rayt's mercs shift their eyes towards each other, careful not to move their heads. Both nod slightly and then drop their blasters to the deck.

"Now you, Rayt," growls G'radian. "Drop the weapon and put your hands down to your side." G'radian waits a heartbeat before saying, "Or would you prefer to test me further, you sniveling coward."

Rayt tenses at the insult but drops his blaster. "You'll pay for this, G'radian. You owe me and my men for the last job we pulled. You've got your booty, we just want our due."

Bolton pulls the blaster out slightly and growls to the two thugs, "It's time for you two to leave. Run, don't walk, back to your ship and wait for your Captain. I have monitors everywhere so don't be stupid enough to come back."

Without any hesitation the two turn and start fleeing at full gallop down the corridor, not looking back. Bolton keeps his blaster leveled on them, knowing all too well they are still dangerous.

When the two turn the far corner, he turns back and levels his gun at Rayt's head. "Now give me a good reason not to splatter your brains on the bulkhead."

The buzzing blade moves even closer to Rayt's trembling forehead. Tiny bolts of green and white are continuously sparking now, each strike leaving a little pit of scorched skin. Rayt is straining to keep his eyes open against the strikes.

G'radian is also straining, trying to resist the impulse to decapitate the Grockna and be done with his stupidity.

"You're the worst kind of thug, Rayt. You think the world is yours for the taking and everyone in it is easy prey." He backs his sword a few inches, never taking his eyes from the merc. "You're the biggest mistake I've ever made and now hundreds have paid for my error."

"What are you talking about, Father?"

G'radian points his bony chin at Rayt. "I just got the word. This bastard didn't follow my usual orders for the raid. His ships were supposed to disable the FTG escort, board the supply ships and make off with any non-essential goods, leaving the ships and crews intact. He's was supposed to take the 'booty' and leave with no loss of life. It's the same gameplay we've always run. The idea is to harass the FTG supply convoys not destroy them."

"You're a fool, G'radian," growled Rayt.

Bolton pressed his blaster hard against Rayt's temple and barked, "Shut up or I'll put a hole in your ear! What happened, father?"

G'radian sighed. "This fool attacked the convoy, destroyed the FTG escort ship and half of the supply vessels. I've only got part of the story, but it's enough to know I'm party to murder now, not just pirating."

He inches the blade forward again and snarls, "My orders have always been to disable the escorts, take the supplies and leave with no loss of life. It was making you and your crews rich! Why the hell did you do this? What profit is there in it for you?"

Struggling to keep his body still but raging inside, Rayt manages not to lean forward into his captor. "You're a fool, G'radian. The supplies are nothing. It's the slaves that matter. I can get ten thousand credits for each body I deliver to the Karsh slave

Guild. Triple that for an FTG officer." Rayt can see the shock in G'radian's eyes. He leans back, his booming laughter echoing in the hall. He leans forward again, daring the blade to touch him. "I've been taking any bodies I can grab before we leave the ambush for months. You never knew." Emboldened by G'radian's stricken face, he pushes again. "I'll be heading your little project soon, you weak fool. My lads will be back with reinforcements and we'll take you both down."

"Damn you, Rayt! The only revenge I seek is with the officers on the Eleusis, no one else and you knew this! Your greed has destroyed everything." In one swift movement, G'radian slams the side of his blade against the merc's temple, dropping him like a bag of bricks.

"Bolton, shove that bastard into the hall while I grab our escape gear. We've got to leave, now!"

Bolton holsters his blaster and starts dragging the heavy Grockna out of their small nook. G'radian pops a panel and grabs the 'escape' pack, already stuffed with credits, weapons and essentials.

"We need to get to the ship before Rayt's goons find us." G'radian hesitates and puts a hand on his son's shoulder. "I'm sorry, son. You were right. My grief and obsession has put us here. I have to make this right somehow, with you and with the FTG. I hope you can forgive me."

Bolton nods. "We both need to make this right, father. I didn't stop this, so I am as guilty as you." He palms the destruct button. "Let's go, we've got sixty seconds before this blows."

Bolton checks the outside camera. The hall is clean except for Rayt's body, spread eagle on the deck. "It looks clear."

He presses the door stud and starts out the room. He takes two steps and grabs his back, and screams. G'radian steps through the portal looking down at Rayt's grinning face, his arm extended. G'radian jerks his head to his son's back, where a small red dagger hilt protrudes, blood already starting to drip from the gash.

G'radian's howling blade seems to leap from his sleeve, slicing down and removing Rayt's shoulder and head from his body, digging deeply into the decking. The blade snaps back into his sleeve, smoke trailing behind.

G'radian leaps towards his son's collapsing body, catching him just as he crumples to the floor, eyes closed in a grimace. He holds his son off the deck, careful to keep the dagger from going deeper. "Bolton! Bolton!"

He gets no response. Bolton's breathing is shallow. G'radian feels for a vein and finds only a weak pulse. He lifts his son and starts towards their ship as fast as he can run.

Blaster fire ricochets off the corridor just as he turns the corner. Rayt's goons have returned.

Just as the mercenaries round the corner the destruct blast from G'radian's nooks blows metal and flames directly in their path. Those that aren't incinerated immediately are forced back down the corridor.

G'radian knows his son is lost unless he can get him to the medidoc on their ship. He looks down at his son's pallid face, grief gripping his heart. His stupidity has killed them both.

Chapter Thirteen

Krmot strides into the dingy bar buried deep in the bowels of Sewer City. He's barely able to control his fear. He is terrified that the course he has chosen will be his doom. But it's a once in a life time chance and he knows he has to take it before some other pirate takes it from him.

He glances around a room full of the lowest creatures in the galaxy. Males, females and some species he's never been sure about. All are his mates, his kind of scum. It's a beautiful sight. Most would kill the merc next to him for the price of the next round at the bar. So would Krmot. He smiles a vile grin, his avarice rising to gird his courage. If he succeeds today, his fortunes are secure.

Krmot feels the rumbling and confusion in the room. He sent out the call to each of them an hour ago, knowing full well that everyone knew about the death of Rayt and G'radian's cowardly flight with his son. Rayt was one of them. Krmot shudders, remembering the stories told about Rayt's way of handling FTG captives. So he was a bit rough around the edges maybe, but still a merc. Everyone hated G'radian, but his contacts made a lot these mercs rich. Money goes a long way towards tolerance.

It's time. Krmot walks up to a table at the front of the crowded bar, kicks a chair out from under a drunken, unconscious Grockna. The grey skinned brute flops to the floor, dragging his mug with him. Krmot climbs up the Grockna's body to the table top, kicking mugs and heads out of the way. Standing up to his full length he is still barely higher than half of the room. He starts yelling at the top of his voice, "Mates! Mercs! Hey, over here! Quiet!"

He eyes the room, ready to make his move, but nothing has changed. Loud grunts and squeals fill the air, and food is flying now, smacking the walls. A steaming bowl full of something with dark green tentacles goes flying past Krmot's face. He's got to get their attention before he loses his confidence.

Before thinking the move all the way through Krmot, pulls his blaster and point it at the ceiling. He pulls the trigger and instantly realizes his mistake. It's pure chance that the bolt ricochets off of a fan right into a barrel of Narn pickles. The barrel burst, sending the squealing pickles careening in all directions.

Every merc in the room draws a weapon, and points it at Krmot's upraised arm. It's only the liquor dulled wits of everyone that keeps Krmot from being incinerated.

"Stop!" he yells. "Don't shoot!" With more bravado that he thought he had in him, he slowly slips his gun back into his holster and holds all his hands up. "Quiet down, you drunken squids!" He glances around the room and says, "No offense to the Squids in the room."

Someone guffaws in back of the room. "None taken you schilmy green bag of bonesh." It's a Squid with three small blasters waving in the air, barely able to remain upright on his tentacles. "Ish my nashural state, don 'cha know."

The tension in the room evaporates, replaced with wild laughter, squawks and barks. Guns disappear and mugs are raised again. Krmot knows that he has seconds to take control before chaos returns.

"All right, that's better. Let's get this done." He turns slowly, fixing his gaze from one side of the room to other. "We're here to mourn one our own. Captain Rayt." The room erupts into a mix of cheers and outrage, each merc yelling his feeling depending on which side of Rayt's good side they were on.

Krmot raises his hands for quiet again but the room refuses to comply. *I either have them or I don't. Might as well find out now.* He grabs his blaster again and raises it high so all can see it. A wall of quiet flows through the room. Everyone is focused now on the little Snsh, most sobering up quickly, others just passing out and thumping to the floor.

He slowly holsters his gun again and nods to the room. "Right. Like I said we all have our reasons to mourn Rayt's death. Some of us will miss the big bastard and some will dance a jig on his grave." Krmot shows his preference by doing a lively dance on the table.

Again the room breaks out in raucous laughter. Most have reason to side with Krmot, having no love for Rayt.

"Get to it, Krmot. I have some serious drinking to do tonight. After a jig of my own, if you know what I mean."

"Right! What's this all about?"

The rumbling continues for a few seconds before Krmot holds up his hands again.

"We need to fix the mess that Rayt and G'radian put us in. All these ambushes just to grab a few supply ships must stop. It's time we organized and started working for ourselves, not worrying about whose heads we bust!"

"What if I don't want to organize, you slimy lizard," someone shouted. "I can take any booty I want right now. The FTG is stretched thin from rim to rim."

"That's right. I can go anywhere I want, take any ships I want and keep the booty for myself!"

Krmot waits a heartbeat and then says, "That's right, you simpleton. You could. And next week we'll be hearing about how your brains, what little you have, were turned into star dust by an FTG cruiser because you didn't know that they were waiting for you."

"Have you forgotten how our mates were picked off, one by one, until G'radian found a way to get intel on all those supply runs. Everything changed. Don't you lot remember? Or has drink addled your memories too?"

A pirate near the back yells, "Yeah, but G'radian's gone, who knows where, taking his contacts with him. And Rayt's dead as well, cut in half by G'radian's cursed green sword."

Krmot brandishes a toothy smile and nods. "That's right. They are gone, but I'm not. And I know all about G'radian's contacts. Now we can organize our ships and wreck holy hell on those supply convoys. No more stupid restraints from G'radian and no more thieving from Rayt. If you want more booty than you can swim in, then join me. We'll be richer than the Overloads of Poch!" Krmot raises his blaster towards the ceiling waving it around. "What do you say, mates? Do you want to get rich? Want can take the best and burn the rest?"

The motley group of mercenaries start screaming and yelling 'Krmot. Krmot.' The froth and liquid from a dozen different kinds of inebriating beverages is flying out of mugs and plates everywhere. Claws and fist are flying, pounding on tables and heads, everyone trying to break something.

"Krmot! Krmot!" The chant gets louder and louder, the cheers echoing in the small bar. Krmot's ego bathes in the glory of the reverberations. *I've done it! I'm the new King of Sewer City!*

Chapter Fourteen

My senses twist like a fly caught in a taffy machine. One last gut wrenching snnapppp and I'm back in the hold of the cargo ship, inhaling the pungent scent of half-digested gnats and sweat. I turn to check on Arlo just in time to get a face full of yuck spurting from my buddy's open maw.

"Jesus, Arlo! Could you at least aim for the back of the bus?" It's all I can do to keep the contents of my stomach from launching across the hull too. I grab a rag from a trash bin and start wiping the sticky goo off my face. "How can you have anything left in your gut, dude!"

Arlo looks across the bay and dips his triangular head a little. "Sorry, mate. This body just doesn't deal with transiting like mine did. Damn!" He hawks up a huge wad of dark yellow and blue something and spits it towards the back of the bay. It smells like fermented whale snot, if I knew what that smelled like.

"Quiet you two, I have to contact Sewer City." She glances back at Arlo's newest gift and wrinkles her nose. "For Auturo's sake, Arlo, was that necessary?" She glances back and forth between us and says, "You two jerks are going to sanitize this ship from stem to stern when you get back! Is that understood?"

"Yes, sir."

"Yes, ma'am".

She turns back to the ships control, her nose still scrunched up like a Cabbage Patch doll. Not her best look, but still damn cute.

"Sewer City control, this is Ty'Col freighter Hyperion, please acknowledge." While Pixie is making contact, Arlo and I start checking our backpacks, making sure we don't have anything FTG'ish that would give us away.

"Hyperion, this is City control. Keep your present orbit, our defensive weapons system has been activated and have a fix on you."

Dang, really? They think a POS like Hyperion is a danger? More likely their 'defensives' consist of a decrepit beam cannon and a pile of last week's garbage they can throw at us. If anyone wanted to attack this dump, and why would they, all they would need is a sling-shot and some pebbles.

Pixie yells, "Back off, Control! Hyperion is a freighter, not a damn FTG Cruiser! Are you crazy? I got no weapons, numb-nuts! All I have is a bay full of supplies to trade or sell and space for outgoing cargo."

"OK, OK. Calm down, Hyperion. I was just following orders."

"Well your orders are stupid! Now. I'd like to land and talk to your quarter master. I have three more stops before I can take this bucket of bolts back home. Can we do that or do I need find another port for my goods?"

"Easy now. No need to get your pants in a wad, Hyperion. Wait one."

Groaning to myself, I can't help but think it's just like life in the Navy! Line up against that bulkhead over there and stand at attention and wait. Wait and wait and wait. Then chaos. Then back to wait. Must be a Universal thing. I start scratching behind my ears and give myself a sharp stab from my claw tip. Ouch! I've got to remember I'm a gigantic killer bunny now. It wouldn't look good on my record to slit my own throat.

"Jeeze, Jake, you drew blood again," says Arlo. It's so weird to hear him talk out loud instead of through his implant or his telepathy. We agreed we should keep our telepathic conversations to a minimum. "Makes you look downright scary though. Not a bad look for you."

"Shut up, you two nit-wits. I think we're about to get the OK to dock."

"Hey, Control. How's that invitation going? Is the quartermaster busy or just drunk again?" Pixie is taking a chance that Quartermaster's are the same across the galaxy. Overworked and fond of mind numbing release.

There is a chuckle on the comm. Seems Pixie's intuition was good. "Bernie's on his way to Bay Three-Three-Three. But I wouldn't tease him about his drinking habits if I were you."

"Got it, Control, thanks for the tip. So Bay Three-Three-Three, then?"

"Correct, Hyperion. I'll send coordinates and light up the doors for you. Any chance you have time to throw back a quick one in the bar before you leave? You sound like a Spritezoid, am I correct?"

Pixie frowns a bit but says, "Well, look at you, Control! Good guess. And you?"

"I'm Gardon, from Larq. Interested in a little conversation and recreation before you boost away?"

Larq's are beautiful, dark orange humanoids, most stand over seven feet tall. They are ferocious fighters and concerned only with seeking pleasure and excitement of any kind. Males and females care only about themselves. They are constantly high from the drugs they create and sell.

Pixie turns in her pilot's chair and looks back at me, the picture of innocence. "What do you think, Jake? It would be a good cover for getting you off the ship." She flutters her beautiful eyes at me, waiting to see if I take the bait.

"That will be a 'Hell No', you spicy wench. Not now, not ever. We'll both stay celibate while I'm gone, got that!" I can't smile without slicing a lip so I just point a razor sharp claw in her direction. "Please?"

Pixie chuckles and turns back. "Sorry Gardon, my Grockna boyfriend back home wouldn't appreciate it. I'm afraid he's the jealous type."

I can almost hear the poor schmuck's eyes popping out at the mention of a Grockna boyfriend. "Uh, sure, no problem, ma'am. I didn't mean anything by that. Besides, I think I'm on duty for another day or two before I can get free. Sorry. Please proceed to Bay Three-Three-Three, Hyperion. Control out."

A soft click and the comm to Sewer City goes quiet.

I wag a claw at Pixie and say, "You've got a mean streak a mile wide, Sweetie. Remind me never to get on your bad side."

"That goes for me too, ma'am," Arlo squeaks.

Pixie lets out a delighted laugh, her voice like liquid honey to my ears. "Men are so predictable. No worries, as you say, Jake. The only man I'm taking advantage of is you. Don't forget that while you're gone."

She turns back and starts slapping buttons and switches again. "Now, let's get you offloaded. The sooner we grab these scum bags, the sooner we can all get back to our friends and our lives on Triumph."

The ship veers sharply towards the 'north' pole of the trading output and speeds towards a blinking cargo loading bay.

*****

Pixie guides the old hauler into the small bay, the rust bucket groaning and pinging the whole time. I swear there is diesel smoke drifting from the back and 10w30 motor oil dripping from the bottom of the ship when Arlo and I slip down the cargo ramp. We make for a pile of boxes that Pixie spotted while she was landing.

We make it just before a side door opens and a squat, crusty-skinned Clk Dar chugs in, a small cloud of grey smoke trailing behind. 'Clk Dar' are sort of steam punkish clockwork beings. No one knows where their home planet is, they keep it a closely guarded secret. Each creature is unique. Some have wheels, some legs or tentacles to move about. The only common feature is the slightly oval head, which houses their incredible clockwork mechanism brains. They are constantly breaking down, and have to repair themselves and their mates. They eat a kind of seaweed and wood bark 'fuel' and are constantly spewing noxious smoke and fumes.

From our vantage point I can see this one is smallish, only about four feet high and rolling around on some kind of tank track feet. He has three tentacle arms and two manipulators on a mid-body that looks like a compacted Cadillac. Above the body, he has the typical elongated head with half a dozen 'eyes' on stalks, arrayed at odd angles.

He's waving all his appendages in different directions as he and Pixie haggle over the cargo. I can barely hear the conversation, but I can tell Pixie is letting him get the better of the deal, shrugging her shoulders and finally nodding yes.

Two more Clk Dar emerge from the same door and start unloading the cargo to the back in the bay. It only takes a few minutes and it's done. "Bernie' waves at the two crewmen and then goes back to talking to Pixie.

The Clk Dar cargo handlers glide towards us and I realize our first mistake. We might be hiding in the outgoing cargo area. We need to be further back where the offloaded creates were taken. Crap!

I can hear Arlo in my head saying, "Dude, don't move! Maybe they won't take these boxes!"

The two steam punk collections of gears start grabbing boxes two deep in front us, their exhaust stacks spewing a foul smoke and hot cinders. How do they keep from setting this ship ablaze?

The cloud is settling around us, hopefully providing some camouflage, but it's all I can do to stifle a giant bunny rabbit sneeze. More and more boxes are disappearing around our hiding place.

The Clk Dar have dumped their crates and headed back down Hyperion's ramp. Arlo and I get as tiny as we can. But instead of coming for more cargo, they swerve towards the front of the ship, passing Pixie and Bernie and then disappear through the cargo hatch.

"Damn," whispers Arlo in my head. "That was too close. I may have left another small gift on the floor."

If the whole bay didn't already reek, I might have noticed Arlo gift. As it was I was trying to mentally block out as much of the smell as possible to keep my stomach intact.

Pixie must have finished her business with Bernie because the little gear head is heading back to the cargo bay door and she is climbing up the ramp.

She halts part way up without looking in our direction and forms a heart with her hands for a second.

"Pixie says to tell you she loves you. She wishes us good luck and says come home soon."

"Tell her I love her, Arlo."

Pixie drops her hands, nods and then walks up the ramp. The claptrap ship coughs into life and starts to rise and turn towards the bay entrance. A second later she's gone and the landing bay is empty again.

The cargo bay main lights go out, leaving us in the dark except for the dim glow from a few yellow safety strips embedded in the deck.

We're on our own.

Arlo and I wait a few minutes just to be sure Bernie or someone else doesn't enter the cargo bay.

I stand up slowly, my muscles cramped from squatting for so long. Bones pop as I stretch my body back into a bunnyish shape.

It's dim in the bay, but I can still see well enough to move without bumping into things. I step out from behind the boxes. Arlo follows, trying not to step in his gift. He looks around and says out loud in his best John Wayne voice. "Well now, Pilgrim, let's find this G'radian hombre and rustle us up some banditos."

He's right. Time to get this party started.

The bay lights snap back on like a flare. Someone bellows, "Stop where you are! Move and you're stardust."

Chapter Fifteen

"Well, this is another fine mess you've gotten us into, Bunny Boy. Just when I thought we were going to get this party started." Arlo is speaking in my head in case someone has bugged this cell. Considering the thick coating of disgusting muck on the floor, walls and well, every surface, I doubt anyone gives a damn what happens in here, but it's better to be cautious.

The Grockna and his goons had come into the bay to retrieve some of Pixie's newly unloaded cargo. Mistake number two on our part. We should have laid low for a couple of hours before trying to leave. Life sucks, but what are you gonna do?

After taking Arlo's weapons, they took us at blaster point deep inside Sewer City's maze of compartments to a holding tank, slammed the barred door and just for spite the big goon spit on my pink hairy toes. He growled something about 'fresh meat'. They all got a big har-har out of that. We've been here for three days. It smells. It's hot. I'm pissed.

I vent a little frustration at Arlo's insinuation. "Why is this my fault? I didn't hear a better idea from you!" We've been getting on each other's nerves all day, wondering if we'll ever get out of this dump. The Clk Dar that brings our food, and I use that term sarcastically, hasn't said a word. It just chugs in, spewing nasty smoke from its top knot, dumps two buckets of blue sludge and a large bottle of stale water near a square slot at the bottom of the door and disappears through the exit.

"For the twelfth time, it was your idea to come out of hiding so soon. Not that I'm counting or anything."

"OK, OK, OK! I get it, bubble butt. I screwed up," snarls Arlo. His skin is pulsing shiny black and dark blues.

Hmmm. I haven't seen that before. Maybe I need to back off just a wee bit. "It's OK, buddy. We couldn't have known the dock crew of this swill bucket would show up so soon. I was pretty sure that crap would sit for weeks before anyone bothered to touch it."

Arlo huffs and rolls his eye at me. "Yeah. I know." He glances around our lovely accommodations at Hotel Pig Sty and says, "We've got to get out of here or we're going to kill each other before we have a chance to start the mission."

"Assuming there is still a mission to start, buddy. For all we know G'radian has already left on another ambush and we're too late."

Arlo shakes his head and rallies a bit. "What a pessimist! What happened to my 'anything is possible' Bunny Buddy? We've been in worse messes than this, Jake. Put on your thinking cap, man. How do we get out of here?"

"Well I could take out that blaster I have hidden up my butt… wait, nope. I left my butt-blaster in my other body." I shuffle a little across the floor, next to the bars. "But we have to do something, Damn it, I hate being behind these crappy bars!"

I can't believe we've done all this only to be stopped short in a metal dungeon! My frustration finally boils over and I rear back, lunge forward and drag my meaty paw across the bars, my claws instinctively extending to their maximum.

Kkkrrrzzanggg! Thud! Shudder…

Arlo and I stare like Democrats who just walked into a red neck bar in Houston. There's an eight foot section of the barred door laying on the deck. My claws are still vibrating like tuning forks in my hand, uh paw, the glowing pale red edges are slowly fading back to normal.

"Sweet Jezebel in the pumpkin patch, Jake! How the hell did you do that?"

My claws slowly retract, singing the hairs on my skin. "Ow, ow, ow! Damn!" I shake my hand as if that would cool it. "That burns, damn it!"

"I don't care if it melts your knuckles, Jake, look what you did!" Arlo steps forward and puts a hand through the gaping section. He turns around and twirls his eyes at me and says, "Please tell me you didn't know you could do that. I'd hate to think you've let us rot in this cesspool for three days when you could have done this." He points to the door.

"No idea, man. I sliced a few punching bags when we were training but I never thought to try and shred a metal door. I doubt the Morph Squad knew it either. Nanel said they couldn't predict exactly how our bodies would morph, there's only so much the modeling can tell."

Arlo steps back and points to the door again. "Well? What are you waiting for, Wally Wolverine? Slice and dice us out of here!" Arlo scrambles back into the far corner and crouches. "Watch the back swing, Jake, it's a little tight in here, ok?"

I steady myself before the mangled bars remaining on the door. Flinging my paws downward and a little outward so that I don't slice my legs, I push outward on my fingers, mentally commanding my claws to extend.

Tiny tips of sharp bone peek out of my paws, barely enough to scratch my butt. Damn. Must be the pressure to perform or the days of confinement. Slinging my arms again only produces another inch of claw. "What the hell," I mutter.

Arlo must have noticed my dilemma because he chuckles and says, "Cowboy up, Jake, you're too loose. Get pissed like you were a few minutes ago. How about this, buddy. How did you feel when that gorilla spat his green snot on your toes?"

That image rushes back in my mind and whole body spasms, my blood boiling. All of my claws, toesies and paws, pop out to their full length. My goblins toenails penetrate the deck at least an inch, anchoring me to the floor. I start swinging big bunny swipes left and right. After a dozen satisfying smacks, I stumble back a step, huffing like a rhino. Looking over my shoulder I say, "That's how I felt, Arlo."

A couple of loud clangs proclaim the result of my anger. Most of the door is lying is glowing pieces at my feet, the remaining metal is bent outward and hanging at an angle.

Arlo steps to my side and surveys the damage. "Uh. Well. Yes. I think that will do nicely Jake." He gingerly steps over the mass of tangles bars and through the hole that was our cell door and turns back to me. "Remind me to be nowhere near you when someone spits on your toes, Bunny Boy."

I start to walk through the hole and almost tumble face first into the scrap metal. My toes claws are still lodged deep in the deck. I tug each foot up hard, ripping up part of the floor. With an effort I will the claws out of the scraps attached to my feet like gnarly flip flops.

I scrunch through the mess of mangled metal and through the hole. All my nails are back in place thank god. "Well that was kinda fun, Arlo. Shall we go find G'radian?"

Arlo just shakes his head and turns to lead us out of the side door. He looks back at the cell, its ruined door and back to me. "That's coming out of your paycheck, pal, not mine."

"Ha, ha. Original. Any idea how we find G'radian?"

The door opens easily. Why wouldn't it, the inmates are supposed to be locked up in the cell. We step out into a dimly lit corridor that leads to the left. No signs, no neon arrows saying 'This way, stupid'. Nothing.

Arlo sniffs the air and smacks his lips. "Actually, yes. There's a bar pretty close I'd say. I can smell stale beer and something like burning insects." He sniffs again. "Definitely not gnats, but I'd say a close cousin." He points down the hallway and starts forward. "The perfect place to ask about pirates, eh, mate? And grab some real food. I'm starved."

"When are you not starved, Arlo? Fine. Lead the way Kemosabe."

We wind through the corridors, moving deeper and deeper into the maze that is Sewer City's bloated belly. Each time we reach a turning point Arlo's super snout guides us closer to our goal. We hope.

We finally turn a corner where the hall dumps into a main artery of some kind. There's normal light, the sounds of a crowds heard throughout the Galaxy and the smells. Smells of burning food. Smells of the sweat of a hundred different species. And beer. Even I can smell the sharp tang of brewskies coming from galactic pubs up and down the hall.

Turns out almost every planet that harbors life also harbors some kind of grain or plant that can be made into booze. One of the first things a developing species discovers is how to ferment said gain and create the local whoopee juice. The Universe is a very strange place.

There's a throng of foot, tentacle, hoof and mechanical traffic going both ways. The shear variety of body shapes and sizes is mind boggling. Every conceivable, and honestly some inconceivable, variation of mobile lifeforms are rubbing extremities as they amble along.

Somewhere, the Bureau of Universal Species Creation is having its deca-millennial department meeting on life form creation. "OK, people, settle. Let's see. What do we create today? Ohhh. We haven't done anything with wings, gills AND exoskeleton in, like, eons! Goody! Larry? It's your turn. Let's see what you can come up with!"

On either side of this corridor there are entrances to a variety of bars, stores and who knows what. Your typical trading station mishmash of establishments. From the smells and sounds emanating from most of them I'd say every third one is a bar. Trading post. Pirates. Smugglers. And bars. Go figure.

If I was afraid we would attract attention. I shouldn't have worried. We fit right in with this horde of species from all over the Universe. Bipeds, tripeds, quadrupeds and some dude that would give a centipede an inferiority complex. Where does he buy shoes!?

There is a small herd of two foot high froglike creatures strutting down the way that the crowd is giving a wide berth. Maybe it's the pulsing greenish-yellow pimples that cover their bodies. Ick. Or the smell. That's just nasty.

Most beings are sporting some kind of weapon strapped into holsters and back slings. Some look like they could take down a small army all by themselves. That Hranger doesn't need a blaster; her fangs, claws, horny scales and body like a two thousand pound Sherman tank are frightening enough. All Hrangers are female. The Universe has a weird sense of humor.

"OK, Jake. Pick a bar, any bar. We've got to start somewhere."

There is a loud crash behind me and I barely step left in time to miss another Hranger hurtling through the door behind us. She slides to a stop in the middle of the corridor, getting up a little wobbly, blood dripping from her mouth. She turns to the door with a huge toothy grin. She stomps once, the floor vibrating from the force, rears back and lets loose a raucous, barking laugh that echoes off the walls. She shakes her whole body and starts off down the hall towards another bar.

I turn and look past the ruined bar portal. The inside is packed shoulder to butt, the crowd obviously having a great time drowning their consciousness. Just the kind of place to find smugglers, thieves and all around badass dudes.

"OK, buddy. Let's mingle with the locals and find our guy." I sure hope we find him quickly, we can't stay hidden forever.

Chapter Sixteen

Captain Sprague stands by the flap of the makeshift command tent, watching the rear of a lumbering, wheeled cargo truck as it struggles down the valley.

Shurtz steps up and salutes, saying, "That's the last civilian transports to Tannadoc, sir. Commander Conner reports that the convoy is making good progress. We have twelve crew remaining, ready to leave on the flitter." He motions to the boxy agri-ship squatting in the field to their right. It looks like a tired grey beetle, six stubby wings extended and drooping almost to the ground. "It will be tight, but we've been assured the ship will carry us all." Shurtz shakes his head and adds, "I'll be impressed if it makes it off the ground."

Eva, standing next to Sprague and surveying the ragged collection of ships, huts and lean-tos, nods her agreement with a smile. "You and me both. We should probably stay as close to the ground as possible, Lieutenant, just in case."

Sprague frowns. "Are those really wings? As in 'flapping in order to fly' wings? I thought those were fixed."

Eva replies, "No sir, not fixed. Evidently this flitter uses those wings to hover, much like a rotary winged helicopter used on Earth I believe. It was the only transport left in Tannadoc, sir"

Shurtz shakes his head. "If I find out they had a better vehicle but kept it in the city I'm going to string someone up by their…"

"You'll do no such thing, Lieutenant. We should be happy that we received as much support as we have. This outpost is desperate for those supplies, they've been stretched to the maximum just to stay alive out here. Remember that."

Feeling chastised, the Lieutenant says, "Of course, sir. My apologies. I'll make sure we give them all the help we can while we're here." He glances to the flitter, where the pilot is waving at them. "It looks like we're ready to leave, sir." He salutes and says, "Permission to get the crew prepped for takeoff."

Sprague returns the salute, smiling now. "Of course, Lieutenant." He presses the young man's shoulder and says, "You're doing a great job, Randal. Keep up the attitude and effort, I may need to lean on you and Connor a lot more to get us through this."

Shurtz nods and smiles as well. "I'll do all I can, sir." He turns and start shouting orders to gather the last of the supplies and move to the questionable flyer.

"You know he's going to deserve a field promotion too," whispers Eva. "No good deed goes unpunished, as they say at the Academy." She surveys the field and says, "I'm proud of what our people have accomplished, John. Now we need to get them settled at Tannadoc and contact the Fleet. Shall we go?" She waves to the ship.

"I'm very pleased as well, Eva. And I want to find out who ambushed us and why they destroyed Strantos!" He straightens his shoulders. "I know it's not proper for an Officer to say, but I actually don't care why. It's not going to stop me from kicking their asses firmly up between their shoulder blades."

They move to the ship, stride for stride.

*****

Tannadoc is a collection of granaries, barns and mills, spread outward from the central natural spring water well. Spreading radially out from the center, there are a few hundred homes, mostly ceramic prefabs and stone houses made from a quarry a few klicks away. The stones are a dark pink, sprinkled with black and green flakes of mineral.

Just outside of the town is the power station, where a combination of solar cells, wind turbines, Stirling generators that feed off a tiny volcanic heat vent and a small, ancient fusion reactor supply electricity for the town and the surrounding area.

It took all day to get the over eleven hundred survivors quartered and the wounded attended to in the small hospital. The townspeople opened their homes and hearts to Sprague's refugees, many giving their beds to the wounded and sleeping on the floor.

The town hall does double duty as livestock barn. Currently the animals are outside, packed tightly together in corrals or roaming freely while more makeshift beds are spread around the barn. Sprague, J'Kal and Connor are seated at a large table with the town administrators. A small cask of beer has been tapped, mugs of the warm brew being passed around the table.

"We want to express our deepest gratitude for everything you've done to help us, Mayor Bunaris. We are in your debt, sir. A debt I will personally guarantee is repaid." Captain Sprague raises his mug in a salute.

Bunaris, a big, barrel chested Gruenite, raises his mug and says, "It is our duty and honor to assist in any way we can, Captain." He lowers his mug to the table and looks around the table. "We are saddened that so many of your convoy were lost in the attack." He nods to J'Kal, "Do you know who did this thing?"

"No sir, not yet. We need to contact Fleet Headquarters to start the search for the bastards. I understand you have a communication system but are having some kind of trouble. Are there any other settlements that may have one?"

"No, I'm afraid not. We have the only com system on this moon. We're pretty sure that whoever ambushed you arrived just before you and disabled our system so that we couldn't warn you or call for help. There was an EMF pulse moments before you arrived."

Sprague nods. "That explains our own communications and implant problems. They must have detonated another pulse just as we came out of transit. We have several systems specialist that may be able to help repair your equipment. J'Kal has already dispatched them to your comm hut, we expect to hear from them soon. As soon as they have your system operational we'll ask for immediate rescue."

J'Kal says, "We'll be requesting the fastest transport available for the wounded and some of our crew. The request includes emergency supplies for the colonies here. We need you to contact the other settlements immediately and determine the minimum supplies you can get by with in the short term."

Captain Sprague continues, "J'Kal and I need to return to Headquarters, report and start the search for the cowards. I'm going to leave Lieutenant Connor and most of my crew here to assist you until more transport can be arranged."

"Your help is appreciated, Captain." He rises and signals to the man next to him. "This is Cray, my son and the colony's administrator among other jobs. Cray will work with your Lieutenant. I need to go make those calls to the other colonies about supplies. Please excuse me." The Mayor moves for the door shaking Sprague's hand on the way out.

Connor extends his hand to Cray and says, "Let's put our heads together and see what service our people can be to you, sir." He leads Cray off into the barn to discuss the logistics.

J'Kal's comtat beeps and she keys the blinking tattoo. "Yes?"

"Ensign Zmar, sir. We've repaired the com system. We were fortunate that the system could use the parts we brought from the base. We've make contact with the Triumph, sir. They are the closest FTG vessel in the quadrant. We've asked for a secure channel. They are waiting for the Captain to report."

Sprague nods to J'Kal and starts for the door. "Well done, Ensign. We're on our way."

*****

The communications unit is a simple system, the video is a two dimensional projection display. Captain Starla and her XO, Lieutenant Commander Betzel, are standing next to a console in the Captain's ready room. The room consoles are alive, showing ship status from all departments. The Captain cannot afford to be away from the pulse of the ship, even for a moment."

"Captain Starla, this is Captain Sprague, Strantos Prime. Is this line secured?"

"We have you on screen, Captain, though your transmission is a bit weak. Yes, this is a secure transmission. Fleet thought that your convoy was lost, it is good to see that they were wrong. Please give me a high level sit-rep."

Captain Sprague briefly rubs his eyes to hide his sense of loss. "Yes sir. The short story is that we were ambushed just as we entered the system. They knew exactly where we'd emerge from transit. They detonated some kind of EMF device and then destroyed Strantos before disabling or destroying most of the convoy. It appears they were after bodies more than supplies. What was left of our ships and crew managed to make it the moon settlement and set up a temporary base. We contacted Tannadoc, a local colony, who brought our people into their homes. We are calling from their com hut."

Starla stiffened in anger but controlled her fury at this atrocity. Her voice was tight and controlled. "How many survivors, John? How many casualties?"

Sprague rubs his eyes again, remembering the attack with all the friends and crew he lost in it. "Approximately eleven hundred survivors. Some five hundred missing and assumed taken. It's impossible to get an exact count since we don't know how many were lost in the attack."

"Damn!" cries Starla, in a rare show of emotion. "This is outrageous! If these are the same bastards that have been raiding our convoys then they've turned into murdering thugs. We cannot let this stand!"

A brief moment passes while both Captains draw in their emotions and return to the tasks at hand.

Starla draws herself up to attention and says, "We'll visit this again soon, Captain Sprague. For now, how Triumph can best assist you?"

"Fastest possible transport for myself, my XO and twenty wounded in critical need of medical help. Include an emergency triage team in the first transport. We'll return to Triumph with the wounded. The Mayor of Tannadoc is working with the moon's other colonies to gather a list of urgently needed supplies. Once you have that list you can attend to those supplies."

On the Triumph, Captain Starla turns to her XO and nods. "You have the Con, Betzel. Make sure this transmission remains secured. You can conference our conversation and get things rolling as soon as possible. Keep this as close to your chest as you can."

The XO nods and exists the ready room quickly.

When the portal has closed, Starla turns back to the screen. "I'm so happy you're alive, John. I thought we had lost the Strantos." Small tears flow down her reddened cheeks. "I know we're not together right now but the thought of losing you was driving me crazy."

"I know, Selenia, I know. I feel the same."

With a visible effort Starla gathers her wits and says, "Why the security, John?"

"We can't take a chance that this leaks, Selenia. I don't want them to know we survived. Eventually the word will get out, but we need time to follow any leads before they disappear into the worm holes they came from. Can you squelch this report on your end before it gets a chance to leak?"

"Yes. Betzel and I are the only ones in the know and we'll try to keep the rescue operations hidden behind a false training exercise. XO?"

"Understood, Captain," responds Betzel via their shared implant link.

Again focusing on the video screen she asks, "What leads do you have? I thought Strantos was lost along with most of the rest of the convoy."

"That's correct. We made it moon side in escape pods and a few shuttles. But the device they used to disable our coms might be traceable. I've ordered J'Kal to scan all the available escape craft's logs and sensor readings from our convoy and the colonies com stations. We'll do a sensor sweep of the attack zone when your rescue vessel picks us up. With any luck we'll be able to find out what kind of device it was and hopefully where it was made. Until then I want you to minimize who knows that anyone from the Strantos has survived."

Starla frowns but nods. "That means keeping Headquarters in the dark for now. I don't like it but I agree it's necessary. Whoever the mole is, he's embedded there, and embedded deep. When we find him there's going to be a special party in his honor, but he's not got to like the gifts he gets."

Through her implant, the ships AI says, "Excuse me for interrupting, Captain, but I thought you would like to know that we've deployed the Abborn, our fastest available frigate, to Captain Sprague's position. We received the request for supplies while you were in this meeting. Abborn's eta is six hours."

Starla says through her implant, "Acknowledged, Ship. Well done."

"John I've just been informed that your first transport has been dispatched. The Abborn is in transit and should arrive in six hours. We received the Mayor's list while you and were talking."

"Excellent! As soon as we can transfer goods and load our critically wounded onboard her, J'Kal and I will do our survey of the area and return to Triumph. I can't wait to see you, Selenia. I'll introduce you to J'Kal and we can decide what to do next."

Starla caught the subtle hint about Sprague's possible new companion and smiles. *Always the gentleman, John. I hope you two are happy.*

"I'm looking forward to it. Ship informs me that a supply convoy and rescue ships will be ready to transit to the planet within the hour. Tell the Mayor to send any other requests directly to my XO. See you soon. Triumph out."

She keys the comtat and watches Sprague's image fade from the viewer. Not for the first time she feels the regret of lost companionship. But both she and Sprague understand that duty to the FTG and the billions of beings they protect comes before personal needs. Starla and Sprague had an extraordinarily rewarding relationship for several years, until the needs of the fleet placed them at opposite ends of the galaxy.

Starla taps the console with a manicured nail and smiles wryly. *J'Kal, is it? You had better be good for John, he deserves the best this Universe has to offer.*

Chapter Seventeen

"Sooo. Bar number twelve, Bunny Boy. We have to find a clue soon and I have to find a bathroom. Assuming this place has a bathroom." Arlo's snout does a spastic twitch. "God, I hope the toilet smells better than the bar!" He dry heaves a couple of times and looks at me, his eyes slowly gyrating in opposite directions. "On second thought I don't care what it smells like, I need a corner to spew in."

"Go! Go, man. I'll look around while you puke your guts out. Have a great time."

Arlo fixes both of his beady eyes on me and dry heaves again. "Yeah, right. Thanks for the sympathy, Pinky." His eyes bulge out a bit and he's gone like a shot. Hope he finds a throne to use, but I'm not confident he'll make it.

A quick scan of the room tells me this establishment is pretty much like all the other filthy, crowded drinking taverns we've been in. At the back of the room is a mind-altering-liquids dispensary with a huge Grockna behind the round bar. Holy crap. The barkeep has a crusty black patch over one eye. You've got to be kidding. What is this, a pirate watering hole?

Looking around, I may have been closer to the mark than I thought. Some of the 'clientele' here look like they just stepped out of an Errol Flynn movie set. On second thought, who's to say that some of these characters haven't visited Hollywood in the past? Just sayin'.

I shoulder my fat bunny body past equally intimidating creatures who barely acknowledge me. I get a few grunts and then a squeaky "puTTo!" when I step on a squid's tentacles. I have no idea what that means but I don't stop to exchange pleasantries.

I finally waddle up to the island and put a clawed paw out in the universal sign of 'gimme something mind-numbing, my good man'. Fortunately my collar allows me talk without strangling me, so I can communicate with One Eye and use my embedded credit chip. "I need a fire-buzz, Cyclops. And a blurb-cooler for my master." I point to the corner where Arlo disappeared. "It seems the last bar served us some winky crack-fries."

Cyclops tilts his head slightly, leans slowly forward, putting his massive hands on the bar and stretching his ugly mug to within an inch of my nose. Uh-oh, did I say 'Cyclops' out loud?

In a gravely iceberg voice he says, "Cyclops? Are you making fun of my poor eye?"

"Of course not, friend. On my world Cyclops was a heroic warrior who ripped his enemies' limb from limb and then made a soup from their bones!" It was the best lie I could come up with on the spur of the moment.

One Eye seems to bite on it. He leans back slowly, his granite face splitting open to show two creepy rows of broken, jagged teeth and fangs. Rising up to his full height, he roars "I am Cyclops! Fear me!" He slams his meat hooks on the bar top, rattling mugs around the bar.

The mob of musty mutineers stops mid-guzzle, turning to see who pissed off the barkeep this time. A heart beat later, with no blood spraying, they all turn back to their entertainment, completely ignoring the Grockna.

One Eye waits for anyone to speak up, his face starting to redden.

Before he can vent his rage I raise my right paw, extend my claws and shout at the top of my bunny lungs, "All Hail, Cyclops the

Warrior!" I bring my claws down on the edge of the bar, slicing it off with a 'clanggg' and sending some kind of red booze flying all around. "Hail Cyclops!"

The sight of the red spray must have set the crowd off because they all rise as one and starting shouting and pounding on each other, "Cyclops! Cyclops! Cyclops!"

One Eye's craggy face splits even wider at the accolades of the crowd. He leans down again, eyeing me with what I think is gratitude. Hard to tell when his face is basically a block of granite. He grabs a dirty mug from the middle of the bar, turns around and fills the mug from several spigots, green and red fumes rising from the mug. He turns back to me and drops the mug in front of me, sloshing the mixture.

"On the house, mate."

That's probably the closest this dude has come to 'Thank you' in his entire life. It warms my pinkish heart. A little. Time to see if my karma holds up.

"Cyclops, my friend. My master and I are looking to crew a ship. A 'profitable' ship if you get me. My master has a personal grudge with the FTG."

Cyclops snorts, sending a slimy honker right into my mug. Nice. I wonder if people pay extra for that.

"Who doesn't?" He waves around the bar. "Almost everyone here has some beef with the Fed. And most of them are looking for a ship as well. What makes you think you deserve a billet more than them?"

Before I can answer, Arlo comes stumbling, four footed around the corner. He looks like doo-doo on a stick. He wobbles up to the bar and signals to Cyclops.

"A chocolate milkshake, bar keep. And a bowl of dried garknots, too."

"Don't know that drink. How about a neural-blitzer to settle your delicate stomach?" The sarcasm drips like thick honey. "And we don't serve dead food here, that's disgusting. You want a cup of goobies, that I can do."

Arlo looks up at the smiling fangs and cringes. "Hmmm. I'll pass on the goobies, they squirm too much on the way down. Just the blitzer."

While the bartender turns to make the drink, Arlo taps me mentally. "So what gives, Jake?" He points to the mess I made of the bar. "Those slice marks look like your handiwork. Did the barkeep call you a pink wuss or something?"

"I called him Cyclops before thinking it through. The dainty patch almost made me giggle. He decided Cyclops was a compliment, so I reinforced that idea. It seemed to work, I got my drink on the house. I hope we can get some names from this guy, I can't help thinking that we're running out of time."

The big guy plops a bubbling mixture in front of Arlo. He sets a small mesh cage of wriggling goobie worms down next to the drink. A dozen fat, two headed fingerlings, dark green and oozing a disgusting putrid orange slime, strain at the cage's sides, struggling to get out. Four dozen bulging red eyes on short stalks are swaying back and forth from Arlo and Cyclops. Yikes. These guys know whose coming to dinner for sure.

"Six credits for the blitzer and the goobs." He looks at Arlo with a wicked grin, just daring him to complain that he didn't want the entre-de-wiggles.

Arlo opens his jaw to say something and notices the look. He snaps his trap shut and gives Cyclops a scaly grin. "Of course, Cyclops." Arlo taps the pay stud with his hand, transferring the credits from his chip to the bar. "Thanks."

We're burning daylight here, let's see if Peewee is going to help us or not. I nod to Arlo, I need to let him act the 'master' here.

Arlo puts down his drink and leans closer to the bar. "So, Cyclops. Guido in the bar around the corner said you could point me to a ship who needs a first mate. That true?" Arlo taps the stud again and it pings at some credits transferring. Must have been a big tip because the barkeep looks at the stud and raises the mountain ridge above his good eye.

"Yeah, well. I don't know no Guido but the info is good. I know every merc and ship in the City. What kind of ship are you lookin' for, mate?"

Arlo leans in closer and says, "For one thing, one that's not afraid to get up close and personal with the Feds. I've got a few scores to settle with the Triumph and Captain Starla. Big scores."

"The Triumph, huh? What did you do to piss off lady Starbutt?" He chuckles and says, "They say she can shove a torpedo up your nacelle from ten thousand klicks before you even know she's there. Bitch has torched more of my mates than I can count. What fool do you think will tangle with her?"

Arlo nods his head. "Yeah, I know all about that hag and her reputation. Trust me she earned it. That don't make her Queen of the Galaxy though. She spaced my last ship and half my crew. Our hull was full of booty from a spice mine. I lost everything."

"That's too bad, mate." Cyclops spits into a mug and wipes a dirty rag around the inside, totally ignoring us.

"Yeah, I can tell you're torn up about it. But I hear there's a merc with a whole squad of fighters that's not afraid of any FTG ship. Name's G'radian. Heard of him?"

He stops swirling the rag and focuses his one blood rimmed eye at Arlo. He chuckles for a second and then says, "You gents are late to the party. G'radian and his brat have disappeared. Couple of days ago. Damn good thing too. Half the fighters here and most of the FTG would like to rip them both into tiny pieces and feed them to the wogs." He spits into the mug again and goes back to swirling the rag around and around, just pushing the scum from one side of the mug to the other.

Arlo leans back a bit, caught off guard by the news. "If he had a good squad of fighters and was kicking FTG booty, why the sudden hatred for the two? Did he skim the profits or something?"

Cyclops looks inside the mug, sticks a thick finger down to the bottom and wiggles it around. When he draws it out there's a squirming goobie fighting to get away. One Eye pops the hapless creature in his maw, back end first. The goobie's eyes pop out even further as he disappears bit by bit into the drooling mouth. A final 'scrunch' and he's gone. Cyclops sticks his thick black mucus covered tongue out, pieces of goobie parts still attached and then draws it back in slowly, sheer pleasure on his face. Then he frowns.

"Worse. He was weak. His orders was to just damage the convoy ships, not blast 'em to pieces. He just wants to kick the FTG in the balls. They wasn't even supposed to take slaves. G'radian is a wuss and he showed it, over and over again." Cyclops spits a few tiny eyeballs on the floor and curses. At least I think it is a curse, hard to say. "All those FTG maggots just sittin' there, ripe for the pickings. G'radian just lets them go. It's stupid and it finally caught up to him."

My hairy ears pop up at little. I ping Arlo with a look. He says in my head, "This doesn't sound right. Maybe our Intel is missing something. We need the rest of the story, Jake. Hang on to your furry butt."

Arlo shifts again, pushing the cage of squeaking appetizers a little further down the bar. "Yeah. He doesn't sound like much of a pirate to me, either. I thought he was supposed to be some badass gangster! So what happened to him? Someone push him out an airlock?"

Cyclops squints through his good eye. "Someone will when they find the cowards. Word has it Rayt and his gang were supposed to take G'radian out and take over his operation. Rayt ended up in two pieces on the deck. G'radian and his son ran like cowardly nibbits. No one knows where. Yet. We'll find them though. Rayt was a low life scum bag, but his crew was always the best paid in the City. Rayt had no problem grabbing bodies from those ambushes and selling them on the slave market. His crew was getting rich."

Cyclops rumbles over to a customer down the bar, tiny little popping sounds coming from the deck as he steps on the goobie guts.

Arlo spins his eyes and spits a little gooey something on the floor. "Well that's it, Jake. The pooch has been toughly screwed. We have to find a way to contact Triumph and get the hell off this cesspit before something else can go wrong."

I can't believe our crappy luck. Even if we knew where G'radian went, what difference does it make? He's not the leader of the merc squad that's been ambushing FTG convoys anymore. We missed our chance by days.

"Right. We're a day late and a bazillion bucks short." There is no way we'll be able to figure out who steps into G'radian's shoes or even if someone will. This sucks. "We may as well…"

"You two numb-nuts still interested in signing on to a merc crew?" Cyclops moves pretty quietly for such a big brute. He's acting all nonchalant, twirling the rag into the same mug. I think he's grinding in the goobie guts just for the fun of it.

"Maybe," says Arlo, just as nonchalantly. "Depends on how many Feds I can destroy and how many slaves I can nab. I don't want a ship captain that will leave booty drifting in space."

One Eye grunts his approval and points his massive chin to the Clk Dar moving up the bar towards us. The creature is trailing a line of dark blue sticky oil on the deck. A dark haze of fumes surrounds his spiky head. "This is Woktok. He serves on the 'Crak Toh'. He's looking for first and second mates for his Captain, Krmot the Snsh. Seems Krmot has grown a set of big ones. He's claimed command of G'radian's operation."

Woktok's head spins around a couple of times, spewing something icky from several ports. He settles two black orbs on Arlo and me. A voice that sounds like a metallic marimba played at super speed. "Yesss. Looking quicklyyy. Neeedd find quicklyyy. You bestestttt? If lie, Krmotttt will roastttt you and then spaccce you quicklyyy." His head spins a couple more times. "Well? Need ttto know now, must getttt back to ship in one hourrrr or be lefttt behind!"

Woktok's head actually bounces up and down a few times, spewing more ickyness on my pristine pinkness. Gross.

Arlo doesn't bother to check with me first, he slams a fist on the bar and laughs. "Damn right we want the billets, you clanking muck factory. Where's your ledger, mate? Where do we sign?"

The spiky head bobs a couple more times. "Done anddd done, mates!" A slot opens in his chest and a little arm extends. Before either of us can react, Woktok has jabbed us with a syringe looking device.

"There. No sign lleedddger. DNA bitttts will traceee you."

"Hey, wait! What's our cut, you mucked up metal malfunction? We're not signing up for scraps, you know!"

Woktok's head spins like a top and then stops, almost knocking him over from the inertia. "No scrappsss, bone-bag. Captain's cut is half. First and Second Mate split a quarter. The rest is splittt even by the crrrew." Woktok clanks forward to face Arlo, raises his oily face and hisses in a low voice. "You luckyyy. We on our way to ambush convoyyyy now. Pleentyy of boottyyy there will bee."

Woktok does an about face spin saying, "You reporttt bay three-ten before ship's clock twelve hundred." He stops and looks back to us. "If you smarttt, you reporttt quickerly. Krmot is nottt a waiterrr type." He sputters off, changing gears as he gains speed going out the bar.

"Looks like you two are either really lucky, or really unlucky. Hard to say which, if you get my drift." Cyclops has a nasty smile and has stretched his mitt, palm up, towards Arlo. "I believe you owe me a connect fee. I think five hundred credits should make us even."

"Five hundred credits, are you out of your ..." Arlo stops in mind protest when he sees One Eye's other hand resting on a nasty looking blaster on his hip. "Hmmm. Yes, I think that's more than fair, Cyclops. Sure. Here."

Arlo taps the pay stud again.

"Let's go get our gear," says Arlo loud enough for the bartender to hear. "We have to settle with the City Master before we can leave." We don't have anything to settle but One Eye doesn't know that. Arlo eyes the cage of quivering goobies and scoops it up. "I think those credits should cover a little treat for the road, Cyclops. What do you say?"

Cyclops just chuckles and waves a hand. "Whatever, rube. Five hundred credits will keep me in goobies and booze for a month."

Arlo and I step lively out the bar and turn down the corridor.

"Let's get away from this bar quickly, Jake. I don't want Cyclops to rethink his bonus. That rolling tin can said it's another ambush! We need to warn Triumph." He points to a display on the far wall and says, "Let's check that data tablet for a City diagram. We need to find Bay Three-Ten and then we'll see if we can get word out to Triumph before we have to leave."

"Let's find a cosmic telephone somewhere and make a collect call." He turns and walks towards the display on the far wall.

Arlo steps up to the screen looking for directions and then points to the left. "OK. Bay Three-Ten is ten minutes that way. The map shows a communication booth just down the corridor. Let's see if we can make contact without getting our asses caught calling up an FTG ship."

Arlo starts off at a brisk waddle. I grab the cage to keep it from flying around and take off after him. The traffic is thinning quickly. All the bars must be back the way we came.

Turning down the next corridor, we step to the side. There's almost no traffic. There are only a few doorways on either side. Half a dozen drunks are slumped against the walls, drooling and muttering drunk songs. You know, "She done me bad, but I had a great time," sort of songs. Arlo stops half way down the corridor and steps into a small alcove. There's not enough room for both of us so I stay to the side.

Arlo looks at the console and says, "OK. This comm looks like it's working and has a pay stud. I think I can make a directed call from here. We've got to assume in a place like this that someone will be monitoring outgoing transmissions so we'll have to bounce the message through a few of the FTG relay stations to throw them off for a while at least. We've got to get a warning about the trap to Triumph without raising any immediate alarms here. Any ideas?"

Actually, for once, I did. I glance up on down the hall. No one was moving, so I grabbed the drunk behind me by the hand. "We make the call on this guy's dime. That should confuse the hell of them. I've got an idea for the message too. Send this…"

After we send the message, we put our pay-pal back up against the wall, but not before Arlo snags the brute's blasters and knives. Then we boogie to our rendezvous. Along the way, I can't help but wondering how we're going to stop the ambush without blowing ourselves up as well.

I'm wracking my brain trying to come up with a good scheme. But every idea stinks and is pretty much sure to fail, ending with our FTG friends being trapped and blown to smithereens. This mission is going down the tubes faster than a politician can flip-flop during a campaign.

"I sure hope that works, Arlo. I can't sit by and let another convoy get destroyed. I'd never be able to live with myself." Arlo knows where I'm going with this.

Arlo grasps my arm and squeezes it. "I know, Jake. If Triumph doesn't show in time we'll have to take the ambush out ourselves somehow. We'll figure something out, I promise."

The next bend opens up to a series of launch bays on the right. We must be close to the outer hull, where cargo ships enter and leave. Foot and bot traffic is heavier here, crates of goods flying around in what looks like total chaos.

The third bay ahead has "3-10" glowing in dull red letters above the yawning mouth of the hold. There is a B'Rovian fighter inside, squat, ugly as sin and bristling with armament. It's taking up almost a third of the space. The access ramp is down, crewmen hustling up and down with crates of all sizes and shapes.

Inside and just to the left of the bay entrance there is a group of scummy looking crewmen lounging at a bar. A bar in a launching bay. OK, being a scumbag does have some pretty cool perks. There's a Snish in the center of the group. Aargh, there be pirates here.

"Arlo, that's it. I think that's our Captain at the bar. Let's get the ball rolling here. We need to go into master/slave mode again."

"Roger that, BunZilla. Stay behind me and keep quiet." Arlo puts up a hand and says, "I apologize now for anything nasty I may have to do to keep our cover, Jake." He starts out without waiting for me.

I start after Arlo and yell, "Wait. What nasty thing?" Oh crap. A jolt of white lightening plays up and down my spine and I scream out loud in pain.

We're close enough for the Captain and his entourage to have heard my yelp of pain and they all turn to watch us.

"Shut your yap, slave!" barks Arlo. "You'll get more than a love tap next time."

Arlo stops a few feet from Captain Krmot's stool and slaps a fist across his chest. That's the way all the bad guys salute in the 'B' movies, so hell, why not?

"Captain. I'm Kong and this is my pet. I call it 'BunZilla'. Your Clk Dar, Woktok recruited us, so we're reporting for duty, sir." Arlo bows slightly and then stands upright again. It never hurts to puff up the ego of your potential boss to distract him. In this case, it works like a charm.

The Snsh stands up off the stool, a superior smile on his ugly face. He gives me the once over and says, "Your pet looks like it could hold its own in a match, Kong." He raises his eye ridge and says, "Which is good for you. I need a first mate. Woktok said you've got experience." He looks at me again, his froggy eyes sliding over my pink, wrinkly body. I feel so dirty and violated. Ick.

Arlo waves a hand at me and nods. "I've won my fair share of matches, Captain. BunZilla is ugly as sin but he can take a beating." Arlo gestures around the crowd and says, "When we get back, I'd like to set up a match and do some betting."

Krmot slams a fist on the table and lets out a stuttering hiss of a laugh. "Hah! Woktok has a strange sense of humor, mate. A match is how you get the job, Kong. You put your pet up against my other choice for first mate." Krmot points towards the end of the bar where a Gruenite pirate has a leg up on the bar step and a huge mug in his hand.

Krmot motions for the pirate to join us. While the scurvy brigand makes his way to us, mug in hand, Krmot says, "Crow here wants to be my First, too. So you'll have to put your puff-ball against his pet to get the job."

Crow sidles up to us, nodding the Krmot. "Captain." He eyes Arlo and then me with distain pouring from his mustached snarl. I think it's distain. Could be he's got a mouth full of abscessed teeth. "You can give me that billet now, Captain. This ball of pink fuzz won't last ten seconds with my pet."

He turns to Arlo and says, "Listen, mate, I got no beef with you. Yet. But if you put your slave up against my Herk, there won't be enough left of it to fill a piss bucket. Save yourself the embarrassment and join the boarding crew." He leans against the bar, looks down and spits a thick wad of distain on my foot. Yep. Abscessed teeth it is. I'm really getting tired of being spit on. My talons are itching to spring out and slice this guy a new smirk.

"Easy, Jake, I'll deal with this," says Arlo in my head. "Just be ready for anything."

I force my claws back into their pads and ease back onto my haunches.

Arlo calmly snatches Crow's mug from his hand and smashes it over the turd's head. The mug shatters into a hundred pieces, the booze soaking Crow's beard and hair. Crow and the small crowd of pirates around us are stunned into silence. Crow's face is turning dark red, his eyes bulging from their sockets.

"Keep your drool to yourself, you steamin' pile gath'nar." He tosses the handle to the side and looks around at the crowd that's gathered around us, like vultures to a week old kill. "BunZilla here could crush you like a bug with his little finger." He smiles and looks at me. "Show him your best smile, my pet."

I lean forward and up over Crow, slowly opening my maw and extending my quiver of shark teeth. It's my turn to drool. Saliva dripping from my bottom jaw onto the boots of the thug. I lean forward a little more and open my mouth a little wider, inches from his suddenly pale face.

A little jolt of electricity hits my collar, causing me to snap my mouth shut and to rock back onto my haunches again.

"That's enough, slave. We don't want our 'mate' here to wet himself before the match is over." Arlo adds in in my head, "Well done, Dude. I thought you were going to take his head for snack!"

Krmot starts hissing and slapping his thigh, obviously enjoying this scene. On cue, the crowd burst out laughing too, several of them yelling there approval. "Hey, I'd pay a month's credits to see Crow piss his pants. Do it again!" The crowd erupts in laughter again.

Huffing, puffing and spraying the brew from his beard, Crow is starting to build up a full head of steam. Oh, my. His neck and face are turning a lovely shade of eggplant purple. He starts for his blaster. *Crap we went too far!*

Krmot grabs Crow's hand before Crow can draw the weapon. "Easy, Crow, easy. The boys are just having some fun."

Crow looks like he wants to just shoot us anyway. Some of his comrades start slapping him on the back and making more fun of him, but it seems to break the tension. He finally wipes his face and slings the wet over his head at his mates.

"Fine. Fine." He fixes Arlo with an evil eye and growls, "You and me will settle this later. Mark my words."

Arlo spins his eyes in different direction a few times, lasers them right back at Crow and gives his best John Wayne. "Well, Pilgrim. Any time you want to lock horns, you can meet me in the barn. Bring your pitch fork, 'cause you're going to need it."

The crowd goes quiet. Ugly puzzled faces everywhere. I try to contact Arlo and say, "Uh, partner. You might want to make that comment a little more pirate'ish. You're confusing the natives."

"Oh. Right. Good point," he says back in my mind.

He scans the crowd and then Crow and growls back, "Anytime, Crow. Anytime."

Krmot claps his hands and shouts, "Fine, fine. You two can beat each other senseless for all I care. Just do it after we're back. Right now, it's time to see which one of you is my new First Mate and which becomes a deck hand."

The crowd lets loose with a cheer, obviously ready for a fight, no matter who the combatants are. Some guy to the right is already calling for bets. What the hell, he doesn't even know who is fighting. Hmm. He's grinning at me and making twig snapping motions. That can't be good.

Crow says, "Yes! It's time for your powder puff to meet Herk." He touches a stud on his wrist control. There's a horrible, wailing scream from behind the crowd. The crowd instantly splits down the middle to reveal 'Herk'.

Oh. My. God.

Chapter Eighteen

"Lieutenant, may I have a word?"

Lieutenant Tillet sets her fork down and raises an eyebrow at the holo suddenly sitting across from her. She wipes her mouth and says, "Of course, ahh, Einstein, isn't it?"

The holo-image is an elderly human. He has disheveled, white hair surrounding a gently wrinkled smiling face. He's sporting a grey, frumpy sweater and smoking a small pipe. The virtual smoke rising from the pipe is forming equations and evolving formulas.

"That's correct, Sweet Cheeks."

Tillet raises both eyebrows at the familiar term and then scowls. "When you're addressing me, avatar, you'll keep it professional. Understood?"

Einstein chuckles and says, "I'm afraid Jake gave me specific orders to call you that, Sweetie, if I should need to contact you on his behalf. I think he feels it is a good security token for our talk, something only he would say to you."

Tillet says reservedly, "I see."

"I've received a message from Mr. Jasper over an unsecure communications link, routed through a dozen of our relay stations. The message was not paid for by Mr. Jasper or Arlo. He obviously doesn't want someone to intercept the message but doesn't have access to a secure comm link. I believe the message is some kind of coded warning."

Tillet quickly scans the room noting several crewmen within a few feet of her table.

"Don't worry about eavesdroppers, ma'am. I've had Ship put a secure electronics curtain around us. If anyone is listening they won't be able to understand anything as long as we keep our voices low."

Tillet looks at the barely visible shimmering curtain of energy dome around them. She might have missed it except for the slight distortion behind Einstein's avatar.

"Very well. Ship, are you monitoring this conversation," she asks.

The ship's AI answers in her implant, "Yes, Lieutenant Tillet. Einstein requested that I monitor and to link your conversation with Captain Starla. She is listening as well, I believe."

Starla's voice is anxious in Tillet's implant. "I'm listening, Lieutenant. Proceed."

Tillet nods to the avatar and says, "Let's have it, Einstein. When did you receive the message and what does it say?"

"It was received ten minutes ago by our Communications department. After scanning it for malware, they forwarded it to me. I notified the Ship and then Captain Starla. The message reads: 'Einstein. Tell Sweet Cheeks not to come to the picnic today, I couldn't get rid of the bugs on the hot karc in time, I need another hour or two. We'll try again next week. Same Bat-Channel, same Bat-Time. Kong.'"

Pixie puzzles over the message a moment and then smiles. "Clever boys."

Starla says, "Who is Kong and what is he talking about, Lieutenant? What do bats have to do with the mission? And what does 'karc' mean and why is it hot?"

"Kong must be Arlo, since Jake is supposed to be his pet. He's warning us that they need another week to infiltrate so don't send the current supply missions out. The bat reference is from an old Earth television show Jake made me watch. It is quite a bizarre theater series, but he said it had a huge following. I'm afraid the nuances of the intellectual dialog and esoteric plot escaped me. The reference means to set up the next supply convoys for one week, but in the same locations. I have no idea what 'karc' means though."

Ship says, "I'm afraid some scheduled convoys have already left, Captain. Should I notify Headquarters to stop the others for now?"

A moment later Starla says, "How often are the convoys deploying, Ship. And when is the next group scheduled to depart?"

"Roughly two convoys a month, sometimes three. It depends on the requests we receive and availability of escort ships. The next group is due to depart in 8 days. Three convoys are being assembled."

Tillet says, "Einstein, can you get a secure message back to Jake?"

"I cannot say for sure, Pixie Poo…"

"Wait, Einstein. We've established that the message has come from Jake, there is no need to continue the pet names. It's Lieutenant. Understood?"

"Yes, Ma'am."

Starla chuckles, "Pixie Poo?"

"Excuse me? We can discuss that later, sir." Tillet is turning a lovely shade of pink, almost matching her hair. "Einstein?"

"Yes, ma'am. As I was saying, I can send a message back through the same routes but I have no way of knowing if the message will get to them, I don't know which ship he will be on."

Einstein says, "If I may, they would not have sent a message without giving us a clue as to where to contact him. There must be something in the message we are missing."

Captain Starla says, "I'll leave it to you and Einstein to find out where our team is. I'm going to have to find a way to stop the convoys without raising suspicion and tipping our hand to the bastard that's feeding the mercenaries our plans. Contact me as soon as you have something." Starla's implant goes silent again.

Lieutenant Tillet says, "Einstein, can you analyze the message for other Earth references, particularly with the television and movie shows that Jake would have seen. He must have talked with you about Earth and his past."

"Yes, ma'am. Quite often. Whenever you were on mission Mr. Jasper spent much of his time in our library, watching these shows and talking about how things were 'different in my day'. He had a particular fondness for mid twentieth century 'spoofs' I believe he called them. The 'Batman' television series was his favorite, but there were many others."

"Reanalyze that part of the message for any anomalies, misspelling, and other references. Jake would have to disguise his destination but not make it impossible for us to decode."

"Yes, ma'am. I'm running each word and phrase again. Processing. Processing. Processing."

"What is the point of saying 'Processing", Einstein? I know you're processing."

"I'm sorry, Lieutenant. Mr. Jasper had a fondness for another television series of that era that had an AI that used that phrase."

Tillet shakes her head wearily. "With all that trivia baggage filling Jake's head it's a wonder he can function at all."

"I agree, Lieutenant. A discussion for another time perhaps. I may have found an anomaly in the message after all. It may have been unintentional though."

"What is it?"

"It's the double 'Bat' phrase reference. The order does not match the archive examples I have."

"How?"

"The proper order would be 'Same Bat-Time, same Bat-Channel'. It is reversed in the message. This seems unlike Mr. Jasper, his phrasing has always been per the archives record."

"Reversed? Backward. Out of order." Tillet snaps her fingers and says, "That's it, Einstein. Reparse the message for each word and phrase in that sentence. Reverse the order of each word and phrase and compare the words to the ships records for vessels known to hanger at Sewer City."

"Processing. Processing."

Einstein goes silent and then a moment later, "I believe I have a match, Lieutenant. The phrase 'the hot karc in time' reference. If I reverse 'hot karc' it becomes 'Crak Toh', a supposed freighter that the FTG has identified as a possible mercenary vessel. It was known to be in the area of several raids on FTG outposts. The local authorities have been watching it. The records show its captain is a suspected associate of G'radian."

"Ringo!" shouts Tillet. Several crewmen at the next table turn to see what the excitement is all about. Tillet raises her glass, downs a big gulp and says, "Ringo! It means great beer!"

The crewmen look at each other, shrug and raise their own glasses. "Ringo!" "Ringo, sir!" They go back to their meals impressed by Tillet's knowledge of beer.

Einstein chuckles and says, "I believe the phrase you want is 'bingo', sir. Ringo was a world famous actor on Earth and Captain of the Yellow Submarine fleet during the Battle of the Blue Meanies…"

"Got it, Einstein. Bingo, then. That's got to be it. We need to get a message to Jake on the Crak Toh. It needs to be simple and not raise suspicions." Concentrating on her conversions with Jake she tries to piece together a suitable response.

"I have it, Einstein! At least I think it will do. Send this message to Jake through the same routers. The message hinted that he wouldn't be on the Crak Toh for two hours, so delay the message for three hours just to be sure."

"Shall I inform the Captain of this before I transmit?"

"Yes. If she confirms the action send this message…"

Chapter Nineteen

"Uh, Arlo? I think someone spiked that last beer we had. Herk looks exactly like…"

"Captain Starla." Arlo's voice whispers back in my head. "Oh, frog nuggets, Jake. It can't be Starla. Can it?"

Can't-be-Starla-but-sure-looks-like-her is striding slowly through the crowd towards us. She is wearing a dull black tunic, laced with chain straps and covered with small spikes. Her pleated black skirt hangs down to mid-thigh, just above the laced, interwoven bands of her boots. On each wrist she has a dark metal bracelet. The Roman Centurion look is killer on her. Literally.

Her body is covered in scars from head to toe. An angry red line runs from her right thigh, under the skirt and tunic and across her left shoulder. A recent wound, not fully healed. No rejuv for slaves I guess. Bastards! She has two narrow swords arrayed diagonally on her back, the hide covered hilts just visible over her shoulders.

Around her throat is the 'obedience collar' and a small red scarf. Her brilliant white hair hangs in dreads down below her shoulders, tipped with red leather ties. She has painted dark kohl around the upper eyelids with a swoop line extending from the lash line halfway to her ears. Her lips are colored with a dark, smoldering red lipstick. A thin, swirling bright green spider web tattoo extend from her right shoulder and up under the right side of her neck to her throat.

Her face is a vision of hatred, her mouth thin and stretched tightly, her eyes red-rimmed, cold and very, very angry.

Crow slaps Arlo on the shoulder and waves at the advancing warrior. "What do you think of Herk, Mate? Aint she a terror?" He taps his control causing Herk to wince and stop suddenly in front of Crow. "A little hard to control sometimes, too. She still fights the collar every chance she gets. I bought her from a slaver in the Godel quadrant. He claimed she'd never been fully 'trained' and never lost a match. He was right on both counts. She's won sixteen matches for me. Now she's about to win number seventeen." Crow laughs at his own words and turns to Krmot.

He slaps Herk on the shoulder and says, "Well, Captain. I've got my pet and he's got his. Let's get this match done so I can grab my First Mates billet and watch this lackey dive into the engine room bilges."

Krmot pokes a finger in Arlo's chest and demands, "Well? You putting up your pet, Kong, or does Crow win by coward's default?"

Arlo rises up a foot and bristles like a porcupine. "I'm no coward, Captain. I don't care if Crow's pet is Zena, the Warrior Princess, BunZilla can take her. Let's do this."

Krmot motions to the center of the bay. "All right, mates, let's clear the area and set up the rings. Woktok will hold your wagers till the fight is over." The crowd starts cheering and moving to the center of the bay. Woktok is suddenly surrounded by eager gamblers of all sorts.

I contact Arlo and say, "Sweet Josephine, Arlo, what do I do now? That has to be Starla's twin or mom or hell it could be her daughter for all we know, considering how they rejuvenate! I can't kill her. I'm not sure I could have killed any pet, but I know I can't do this."

"Yeah. We're screwed. Again. This Universe needs an enema. Seriously it does. We can stall a few minutes. I'm going to try to contact Herk. Act natural." Arlo starts off towards the moving crowd.

Act natural? You've got to be kidding. I'm about to get into a ring with a killing machine that looks just like my captain and try NOT to kill her or get killed myself. What the hell is natural about that!

Arlo and I stand to one side of the arena that the crew are building from cargo crates and some kind of poles with glowing spheres on top. Arlo seems to be concentrating on Herk, as if willing her to do something. Suddenly Herk jerks her eyes to Arlo and then to me. Then she jerks them back forward, looking at the crowd. She hasn't moved a muscle except for her eyes.

"I think we may have our first grain of good luck, Jake," Arlo sends me. "Kasha is Starla's sister alright. I was able to convince her we're from the Triumph undercover. I'll give you the full story when I can. Right now, the fight is about to start. We've got a plan. It's not a great plan, hell it's not even a good plan, but we think it's the only way for both of you to come out alive."

"Great. Terrible. Nuts. Great that we've found her. Terrible that she's a slave. Nuts, what have you two cooked up? I just know I'm going to regret this."

"I guarantee you are, Buddy. I'm sorry but you're going to have to lose something very dear to you. Just fight, stay alive and when I give the word slam Kasha to ground and get ready to run her through with your claws."

"Wait, do wha…"

"Fighters, into the ring," bellows Krmot. The crowd parts enough for me to move up to the ropes. Only they aren't ropes. They're some kind of energy beam, running from corner post to corner post. The air is sizzling and crackling with the energy.

"Oh, I forgot to tell you. The ring uses blaster beams instead of ropes. If you touch one you'll be fried bunny meat on a stick. So try real hard to stay away from them," whispers Arlo.

I think I just tinkled a little on the floor.

Krmot presses a stud on one of the posts and the beam for that side disappears. He motions me and Kasha into the ring and then energizes the arena again. He turns to Crow and Arlo and says, 'It's a grudge match, mates. No rules. First fighter on the floor for three seconds is a loser. If your pet happens to be killed by 'accident', tough luck. Owners can call the match at any time, but then they forfeit the match. Any questions?"

Arlo acts nonchalant, waving at the ring. "I believe the Captain mentioned something about wagers? I'll put up ten to one for my fighter. All bets taken. Any suckers in the crew?"

Arlo pings me, "That should put a bee up their butts, Jake. We need all the distractions we can get."

Arlo's wager draws a wild round of additional betting, everyone trying to get a piece of the action. We're surrounded by booze and credits flying in all directions, everyone fighting to get to Woktok before the fight begins.

"Holy shi.., ten to one? Arlo, have you lost your mind. I may not make it out the ring except in a bag of diced bunny parts. Kasha has two friggin' swords!"

"I've got faith in you, buddy. Plus you have a dozen swords to her two. What could go wrong?" he whispers back. "Just don't go too easy on her, Jake, it has to look convincing."

Before I can return a suitable barbed response Krmot yells. "Fight!"

Suddenly my world goes into slow motion. I hear terror can do that to you. Damn, there goes that weak bladder again.

Kasha's scream paralyzes me for an instant. She's jumping straight at me, both swords swinging forward to slice my head off.

Purely by instinct my wolverine claws extend by themselves and block the blades, glancing them off but taking a half pound of flesh from my right hand. Blood arcs from the wound, splattering the beams, exploding into smoke and fried bunny blood.

I shove my head forward and nail Kasha in the chest. She flips backwards and lands on her feet, clutching the front of her tunic. She takes a deep breath and starts forward in a fighter's stance. Her right sword is extended, her left sword is held back, parallel to her right arm.

She takes another flying leap and ducks under my swipe this time. One of her blades cuts a chunk out of my kneecap, sending more blood spraying into the crowd.

My wounds hurt like the devil. The skin around them is clotting quickly, the blood fountains slowing down to a slow drip. Thank you bio-nerds back on Triumph! I'm not going to bleed to death on the first hits.

To hell with this shit. I open my mega-mouth and let out a wail of my own. Jesus, I sound like Godzilla! Kasha stops in mid step, gaping at the mass of teeth and cavernous maw that is my handsome face. When I stop the yell I purposely slam my jaw shut, sounding like two granite rocks slapping together.

Kasha only hesitates a second. She gathers her swords back into position and starts for me again, maybe a bit slower and with a little more respect.

"Jake, we need some more show. Do something impressive, man! Stop being a wuss!"

You've got to be kidding! Fine!

I extend my feet talons and dig straight into the decking, penetrating it at least three inches deep. I yank a foot up and bring a ragged chunk of plating with it. I toss the metal up in the air and swipe it with my left claws. Clanggggg! The plate parts into three pieces that go flying towards Kasha.

She ducks two of the pieces and chops at the third, deflecting it but getting tagged on the shoulder, her blood adding the mess on the floor. The shrapnel goes flying into the crowd, mowing down a dozen mercs. One piece hits a beam, exploding into a hundred red-hot fragments that cuts a swatch through another section of pirates.

"Jake, big finish coming up. Let Kasha take her prize then step on her!"

"What prize…" Kasha is on me before I can finish. She leaps into the air, flipping over my head and slicing off the tip of one of my ears. My head explodes in blinding pain. I scream involuntarily and spin around just in time to see Kasha slip on the blood and go to the floor.

Before she can spring up I slam my foot on her back, extending my talons, one on either side of her head. I bring my arm back, claws fully extended, a blood red haze fills my vision. All I can think about is jamming my claws through her back.

"Stop!"

My back spasms, the collar around my neck dumping pure pain down my spine. My scream is real, the pain is unbearable.

"Stop! Step off of her! Stand down. NOW!"

Arlo is at my side, holding my raised arm in check. "We won, slave. It's over."

The haze recedes. My claws slowly retract.

"Get off my pet, you fool!" It's Crow on the other side, pointing a blaster at my head. "Let her up or I'll vaporize your head."

Regaining my wits, I retract my talons and ease my foot off of Kasha. I take a step back and lower my arm. My breathing is slowing but my heart is still racing.

Arlo whispers in my head, "Calm down, Jake. We're this close to be toasted even though you won."

"Zap me again, Arlo, quick!"

I can see Arlo pressing the stud and then the blinding white pain streaks down my spine again. The world goes black and I sink into oblivion.

*****

After a smack to the head, cartoon characters get sweet little yellow birdies, tweeting merrily around their heads. I get ten ton, neon orange elephants. Elephants with Elvis sunglasses, spiked shoes and red tutus. Arrrgghhh. My subconscious needs a few weeks in rehab.

Someone is poking me in the ribs with a sharp stick. "Jake. Come on Jake, stop goldbricking and wake up." Oh, it's Arlo. What a relief. I thought it was an elephant's tusk.

Arlo's gravelly voice vibrates in the air like a poorly tuned bell. The Universe really sucks. "All right, all right. I'm dying but I'm awake. Stop shouting at me. You're going to scare the elephants."

"I don't want to know, Jake. Keep your elephants to yourself. You need to wake up. We've only got a few minutes before I have to report to the bridge. We're leaving to ambush an FTG convoy. It's scheduled to arrive at the 'Pong' colony in the 'PPPq' system in four hours. We need a plan, quick!"

The thought of another convoy being slaughtered helps clear my head. "Right. What happened in the fight, Arlo?"

"We can talk about it later. You won. We're alive. Kasha is alive. Right now we need figure out what to do about the ambush. I'm going to be on the bridge, so there's not much I can do. It will be up to you. I have no idea where Kasha went, but she's got to be somewhere in the crews quarters."

"Were you able to get her story and will she help us?"

"Yeah, sort of and yes, she will help. All she had time to tell me was that she has been a slave for years, being sold or traded whenever her masters lose interest in her. Starla probably thinks she was killed in a raid, but Kasha survived and was captured. She tried to contact Starla, but the collar limits her every move and her masters operated far from FTG monitored territory. Crow keeps her in static mode when he's not around. And Crow doesn't know who she really is."

"What the hell is static mode?"

"The collar basically paralyzes her in place, like a frozen popsicle. She can't move or speak. He leaves her in his quarters until he needs her to fight. We can get more info later. Right now we need a plan."

"OK. Right. How about this. I'll try to find the weapons control and disable it. If I can't disable it, I'll sabotage it to blow up before they can fire."

"Yeah. That was pretty much what I thought. Not much of a plan, but…"

"It's all we have, buddy. I'm not going to let these scumbags murder another convoy. There's no way to contact..."

A panel beeps on the wall and someone says. "Kong. You have a message from some female. Just audio. Said her name was 'Sweet Cheeks'. It's in your quarter's comm unit. She sounded hot, Kong. Care to introduce her to a real man?"

"Yeah, sure. As soon as I meet one on this barge." Arlo flips the comm off and taps the play icon. Pixie's voice is faint, but it's definitely her.

"Hey, Kong baby. You left before I could give you a goodbye kiss, you naughty boy."

Arlo pauses the audio. He looks at me sheepishly for a lizard. "She's just not into you anymore, Bunny Boy. She finally sees me for the Stud Muffin I am." He rolls his eyes.

"Shut up, Arlo. She must have got our message and she's trying to tell us something. I just hope it's not too hard to decode."

Arlo taps the icon and Pixie's voice continues, "I'm going to have a big ol' surprise for you next time we meet, honey bun, you just tell me when and where. I want you to light a fire and blow the place up! All of it, you hear! See you soon, baby."

Arlo taps the icon again and spears an eye at me. "OK. I got nothing out of that, Jake, How about you?"

"I'm not sure. She obviously wants to know where and when the mercs are going to hit next. But she's not telling us to stop them either. It's like she wants us to let the ambush happen. But that doesn't make sense. These thugs will take the high value hostages and goods and then kill everyone else. Why would we let it happen?"

Arlo shuffles back and forth, tapping his noggin with a talon. "I don't know. But we've got to make a call. Do we sit back and let the ambush happen or take the mercs out and go out with a bang doing it?"

Arlo turns to me and says, "I know you feel the same way I do, Jake. There is no way I'm going to let these murderers do it again."

My heart is stuck in my throat. He's right of course. One way or another, these thugs are going to be stopped, permanently.

Thinking frantically, I remember a conversation I had with Triumph's Chief Engineer, Stokes, during my training. Stokes was constantly pushing us to think about testing the ship's boundaries, doing mind experiments of 'what if' on every system. We had an argument about the fold drive and how to override each of the bazillion safety systems.

"We could sabotage the Crak Toh by putting the fold drive pulse-igniter into a feedback loop. The explosion would take this ship and probably half the other merc ships out but the blast field would be contained to a couple of kilometers. I think."

"Uh. You THINK?"

"Yeah, I think. What? You want me to do a simulation analysis first. I'm sure Krmot would let me borrow a few megacycles of the ship's AI!"

"Hey, cool it, Jake. It's just one of those OMG moments, man." He snaps his stubby tail on the deck nervously.

"I know, Arlo, but it's all I've got, man. And by the way, I did get top honors in Fold Drive engineering."

I slowly drag a claw on the bulkhead, digging a deep groove into the metal. The sound soothes my nerves somehow. Then I think back on Pixie's message. I have that sinking feeling you get when you realize none of your options are going to blow bubbles up your butt.

To hell with it. Arlo and I have trusted our instincts more than our brains more than once and it's worked out pretty good so far. So far.

"Arlo, I think we have to trust Pixie on this. She's saying let them ambush the convoy. I don't understand why and I don't see how it can end well, but I don't see another way out."

Arlo nods and says, "I've got the same feeling, Jake. I sure hope we're right."

He steps back and says, "We're done then. I need to send Pixie a message and then get up to the bridge." His finger pauses over the keyboard and he looks at me. "Should we try and tell Starla that Kasha is onboard as a slave?"

"Good question." It just keeps getting better and better. "In for penny, Arlo. We may not get another chance to send a message. We may as well do it."

Arlo nods his head and starts tapping out a message on the comm unit. "GOT 'CHA, SWEET CHEEKS. LET'S PLAY SOME TABLE TENNIS AT PAUL'S PUKY PARLOR IN QUEENS. MEET ME AT TABLE FOUR. BRING THE GODDESS WITH YOU, I'M BRING A NEW FRIEND, KASHA. WE'LL HAVE SOME REAL FUN."

"Well. That seals that deal, Arlo. We're committed now. We've got another problem to think about. How do we free Kasha? Crow has her on a short collar, literally. We could get her killed trying to free her. Hell, we could get ourselves killed if anyone finds out we're trying to free her."

Arlo snickers and says, "So let me recap, buddy. We have to sit back and watch a convoy of innocent traders and their FTG escort get destroyed, and we don't know why. We have to stay alive during the ambush. We have to find a way to free Starla's sister from a bloodthirsty maniac. We have to contact Triumph again and try to set up another trap and then get away, with Kasha, before the FTG destroys the mercs. Is that about it?"

"Well. Yes. That about sums it up. What? Is there some problem, buddy?"

Chapter Twenty

Triumph is floating next to the E'scude system space dock. A small fleet of two dozen supply ships cluster about the dock, shuttles scurrying about loading supplies and readying the convoy. The FTG Frigate 'Goggin' holds guard position outboard the docks, like a sheep dog watching its herd.

The Abborn has barely settled in her launch cradle onboard the Triumph before the loading ramp drops and emergency teams are scrambling up to assist the wounded. Large transit red tiles are quickly filled and begin to zip off at high speed to the medical facilities, their charges firmly secured and surrounded by med techs.

Captain Sprague and Lieutenant J'Kal wait until all the wounded are taken care of before walking down the ramp to meet Lieutenant Commander Betzel. Betzel is huddled in close conference with a human medical officer who is calmly entering data on his comtat. They stand patiently a few feet from the pair until they finish their discussion.

"That's the last of the wounded, Ensign. See to their care personally, Mr. Simon. I want a full report as soon as it's available."

The Ensign taps his comtat and looks up to the XO. "Understood, sir. I've been in contact with Ship and the med labs."

Simon keys his implant and pings the XO. "For your information, sir, the Captain informed me that the actual nature of this 'drill' is to be kept as quiet as possible. Lieutenant Commander Nanel handpicked the medical teams and apprised them of the need for strict secrecy."

"Excellent, Mr. Simon," Betzel responds.

He continues aloud, "The med labs and med teams are standing by to accept the wounded. Monitors show three charges are in critical need of surgery and questionable to survive. I've routed those individuals to an emergency care facility and notified Lieutenant Commander Nanel and her team to stand by. I've routed the others to med labs close by. We'll do everything possible to help them."

Betzel's face clouds at the possibility of losing any of the survivors of the raid. "I'm sure you will, Ensign. Carry on."

The Ensign snaps a quick salute and jumps onto a transit tile. He's gone before Betzel can return the salute. Betzel files a mental note to review Simon's record, he's shown uncommon sense and command attributes that Triumph is in dire need of. Recent fighting has taken its toll on the crews compliment. The Medical department has lost several highly qualified officers and crewmen due to the fighting and to attrition.

Betzel looks around and waves to Sprague and J'Kal. Salutes are exchanged quickly and then Betzel relaxes and says, "It is wonderful to see you Captain, Starla sends her regrets for not meeting you both personally." She turns to J'Kal and says, "Lieutenant. Welcome aboard."

Taking the offered hand to shake, J'Kal says, "Thank you, Ma'am. It's an honor to be here. What can you tell us about our wounded?"

"They're in good hands. Currently there are three headed for the emergency surgery and care lab. The rest are being attended as their needs require. I assure you that Nanel and her teams will do everything possible to save them all."

J'Kal breathes out slowly, feeling as though she's been holding her breath for days. "Thank you."

"Of course. Now we need to get you two to the Captain's ready room for a debriefing. Follow me, please." She steps up onto a white and gold tile that has just landed next to her feet.

Sprague and J'Kal step up behind the XO and the tile lifts. The tile loses no time threading its way from the landing bay and through the interior corridors until it whizzes into the huge central access tunnel of the Triumph. A quick corkscrew turn and the tile is zooming at full speed towards the bridge. The Ship is diverting all other traffic away from their tile so that the path is completely clear. They make the bridge in record time.

Corkscrewing again onto the large bridge, the tile settles just behind the main bridge dais, where Captain Starla is just stepping down to enter her ready room. They enter the room and the portal closes behind them.

Starla and Sprague face each other for a heartbeat and then Starla rushes into his arms giving him a brief but intense kiss. Tears start to flow from both as they struggle to separate. Starla straightens her tunic and turns to J'Kal, her face flushed but slowly returning to normal.

"I'm sorry, J'Kal, that was unprofessional and rude." She looks back into her former lover's eyes and continues. "I thought we,,. I had lost this good man forever."

J'Kal covers her mouth and laughs softly, then says, "No apology is needed, Captain. John and I have no secrets. I know how deep your relationship was and how close you still are. I'm just glad I am able to finally meet you. You've left quite an impression on him. Honestly, I'd like to talk to you about several odd customs John has… "

Sprague shuffles uncomfortably, looking between his two loves and says, "Hmm. Can we perhaps focus on the immediate issue and leave dissecting my Id for a future date? Captain Starla, this is Eva Bonnet J'Kal, my XO. Eva, this Selenia Sol'anotta Starla"

Starla smiles and nods. "I'm pleased to meet you, Eva." Seeing Sprague's discomfort her smile broadens and she winks at J'Kal. "We will compare notes as soon as possible, I assure you."

Her demeanor returns to Captain and she says, "May I have the complete report now, Captain Sprague?" She folds her arms and turns her full attention to Captain Sprague. She listens intently as Sprague and J'Kal retell the events of the ambush and subsequent rescue efforts, interrupting only briefly when she wants more detail on some event.

Five minutes later the trio fall silent again. Starla leans back on the console behind her, her face and manner tense and very, very angry.

"Damn! Curse their disgusting hides. All those innocent civilians. And your crew, John! This is bloody war!" Starla stands again and tries to regain control of her emotions.

J'Kal says, "I understand, Captain, but we all know that the FTG does not interfere with local politics or the policing of criminals. At least not officially."

Sprague says, "Eva's right, Captain. Besides, all our intelligence up to now has been that the mercenaries are after supplies and not slave trade. I'm assuming this is the first time they've changed their tactics from harass to destroy?"

"Yes, it is. Headquarters would not have sent you into a combat scenario otherwise. We've temporarily halted resupply missions until we can form a plan to protect the convoys."

Captain Starla considers for a moment and then says, "Captain. Lieutenant. The following information is top secret and not to leave this room, is that understood?"

Sprague and J'Kal respond together, "Aye, Captain."

"When word of the destruction of your convoy reached us we decided to launch an operation to infiltrate the mercenary group we think is responsible for these attacks. We believe their ring leader is an Un-Jun named Ryan G'radian. We think he has a base of operations on the trading post Sewer City."

Captain Sprague jerks his eyes to Starla and blanches. "Is that the same Un-Jun.."

Starla raises a hand to stop him. "Yes, John, it's him." She looks to J'Kal and says, "I can give you the full story another time, J'Kal, but for now just know that Ryan G'radian's clan was attacked in error by an FTG ship. G'radian lost most of his family and many of his clan that day. He has a legitimate grievance with the FTG."

She hesitate only a moment, remembering that day on the bridge. "And with me, since I served on the ship that attacked his people."

Sprague nods to J'Kal. "Yes. And his honor code calls for revenge. An eye for an eye. So he's been slowly capturing all the officers onboard that FTG ship during the attack, one by one."

J'Kal frowns slightly and raises a pointed finger and says, "You said 'captures', not kills. Is that correct?"

Starla lets out a sigh of relief. "Yes, thank the Core. His code of honor also prohibits taking life except in self-defense. G'radian has been taking the officers of the FTG convoy escorts and selling them into slavery in the outer systems that allows it. We've managed to recover several of those officers."

Starla continues, "After hearing of your attack I decided to try to infiltrate G'radian's operation and stop it, once and for all. We had two ready volunteers and we've embedded them into Sewer City."

J'Kal tilts her head in question and says, "Infiltrate? Won't G'radian know if your agents are FTG? Their implants and faces would be easy to recognize. Who are these brave volunteers?"

"Jake Jasper and his partner, Arlo the Devastator."

Sprague's face lights up in amazement. "Two of our highest profile sailors? They'll be recognized before they can take two steps on that post! Even if you disguise their faces their implants can be detected with the right equipment."

Starla shakes her head. "No, they won't. We had their implants removed and we had them bio-morphed. They are completely unrecognizable now. Arlo is a high functioning telepath, so they can communicate with each other easily. But without their implants they've had to depend on their wits to communicate with us."

J'Kal blinks in astonishment and says, "Brave men indeed, sir. They've put themselves in grave danger without a means to call for help. I hope I get to meet them someday."

"I hope you get that chance too, Eva. Right now we're not sure of their status. Our operation has taken a dangerous twist and I'm not sure how it will end."

Starla motions to the portal and says, "I know you want to check on your crew and charges. I'll let you know if I hear anything further."

Sprague and J'Kal look at each other, each knowing what the other is thinking. Sprague says, "I've left my people in capable hands, Captain. With your permission, Eva and I would like to help if we can. All we need is a ship and a plan."

Captain Starla smiles and says, "A ship I may be able to arrange, John. A plan? I think this is more of a 'seat of the shirt' operation as Arlo would say. To make matters worse I cannot linger here much longer, Triumph has received orders to leave soon for another combat mission."

She considers for a moment and then presses a comtat on her arm and says, "Lieutenant Tillet, to the Captain's Ready Room. Immediately."

Barely two seconds later a response echoes from her tattoo. "Acknowledged, Captain. On my way."

"While we wait for Tillet, let's put our heads together and see if we can come up with something. Ship, I want your input as well."

The ship's AI replies in the room speaker, "Yes sir."

*****

"It will take several hours to refit the Hyperion at the space dock, sir, I'll oversee it myself. I'll leave you to work out the finer details of the mission." Tillet salutes Captain Starla and turns on a heel, hurrying out the portal.

J'Kal frowns and says, "Ah, yes, the finer details. I've flown a lot of missions, Captain, and this mission has more loose ends than a Baruesian's butt. How soon is your convoy set to launch?"

"They're scheduled to leave at 0800, Lieutenant. But I cannot keep Triumph here any longer to assist. I have to leave immediately. You'll need to coordinate with the convoy and space dock to finish. That gives you and Tillet less than two hours to finish preparations on the Hyperion and get into position. You are in good hands with Lieutenant Tillet, I assure you. She one our best pilots." A small smile plays on Starla's face, "It just so happens she is also Mr. Jasper's companion, so she is extremely motivated to get him back in one piece."

Captain Sprague raise his hands and massages his temples again. "I have no doubt we'll be prepared on our end, Captain. But there are so many variables in this scheme I believe it's going to boil down to luck more than planning. In any case, it's the best we can do. To do nothing would be far worse."

J'Kal agrees, "Yes, far worse." She glances at Sprague and then Starla and says, "I believe the best use of my time will be helping Tillet with the refit. I'll leave you to catch up on old times. Captains." She salutes and exits the portal before either can stop her.

Starla recovers first and says, "Well. There goes a better woman than I. I'm not sure I'd have the confidence to leave my lover in the hands of his ex. She's a remarkable woman, John. How much does she know about us?"

She backs up and leans on the console again, eyebrows raised in question.

Sprague doesn't hesitate, "Everything, Selenia. Besides, it's been a long time since we were together. I'm sure you haven't been a hermit since then, you're far too passionate a woman to sit and pine after a lost love."

"You're right, John. And I'm just as sure you found other hearts to break as well." Her smile softens the jibe, if only a little.

Sprague starts to speak, but Starla raises a warning finger first. "No. Wait. I was only trying to keep it light, John. We're both far too pragmatic to hold grudges. When I was made Captain of the Triumph we both celebrated my promotion knowing it would end our relationship. The needs of the service will always come first for both of us."

Sprague acquiesces, "You're right of course, Selenia. That doesn't mean I haven't missed being with you. Eva is an amazing woman and we're very good together. Even if you and I were possible again, I would stay with her. I hope you understand."

"I understand, John. I would never do anything to come between you, you know that."

An awkward silence ensues for a few heartbeats. Starla stands again and walks up to him, taking him by the collar and leaning in close, eyes smoldering. Then she kisses him for a long lingering moment. Then she steps back and sighs.

"I believe you need to go help with the refit, Captain Sprague. I would prefer it if you and Eva would return with my Lieutenant and ship in good working order." She winks wickedly and steps through the portal, the Captain of the Triumph once more.

Sprague takes a moment to recover from the embrace before muttering, "By the Core, was that hello or goodbye? I will never understand women."

He straightens his shirt and steps through the portal, onto a waiting tile and heads for a shuttle to the space dock. He smiles and thinks, "I guess I'm not meant to understand them, just to love them."

Chapter Twenty One

Krmot's small fleet of four fighters and his own ship, the Crak Toh, are gathered in the system but far from Sewer City itself. Each ship is loaded for combat and standing by to fold, awaiting the word from Krmot to transit to an ambush point.

He leans forward to tap Arlo on the shoulder with an extended claw. Arlo is seated at the helm, just in front of the Captain's chair. "Number One, have all ships reported ready?"

"Aye, Captain."

Krmot keys the communication panel on the bridge of the Crak Toh and says, "Alright mates, it's time to take the booty from right under the FTG's filthy noses. We've received the coordinates for a convoy to the Kutta Mino system. The fools only have one light frigate to guard the convoy of twenty supply ships!"

"We follow the plan, mates. We transit two minutes before the convoy is scheduled to arrive. The locals won't have time to spot us and do anything stupid, like warn the convoy or send fighters."

Krmot keys the communication link again. "Gruber. As soon as you complete the transit, deploy the Pulse Drones and stand by for my word to detonate them. Make sure you're far enough away that the blast doesn't fry your own systems. Do NOT ignite them until the blasted FTG escort has arrived, you slug! Do you understand? The EMP will only be effective for a few seconds and I want every ship in the convoy disabled this time, especially the escort. We almost got our asses dusted last time because Rayt triggered them too soon!"

"Aye, Captain," came the surly reply. "I'll be waiting for your instructions. Just don't be too late to the party again. Sir."

Krmot flares at the insult. "I was not late that time, you bastard! Crak Toh's drive spiked just as we were folding! I'll have your hide for that if it ever happens again, Gruber. Just follow orders or I'll let someone else have first grabs on the booty! You got that?"

Arlo can hear the Gruber's voice tremble, trying to keep his temper. "Understood. Sir." The last word fairly dripping with loathing.

Krmot checks the ship's chronometer and says, "All ships, standby to transit."

*****

"Hyperion, this is Goggin Prime, standby to transit. The convoy will be two minutes behind you. Good luck."

"Confirmed, Goggin. May the Universe smile on all of us," says Captain Sprague.

He turns to J'Kal, crammed into a makeshift co-pilot seat beside him. They are elbow to elbow in the space that was only designed for one. "How's our cargo, J'Kal?"

Eva can barely turn to view the main cargo bay area which has been hastily outfitted with a blaster turret pod on top and a line of bins and tubes leading a row outer hull outlets.

"It is what it is, Captain. Either this works or we're going to be sitting quacks in the field. Is that right, sir?"

"Close enough, Lieutenant." He checks the chronometer. Time to go. "Coordinates entered. Commencing transit now."

Outside their viewport the stars warp and twist insanely and then snap back into place, only they are different stars now. A blue and green planet is hanging in the black of space directly in front of them, but they are alone otherwise.

"Transit complete, Captain. Ready to deploy drones," says J'Kal.

Sprague is watching the ship's clock, beads of sweat forming on his forehead. "We have to time this perfectly, Eva."

J'Kal's hand is hovering over the launch button. "Say the word, sir."

Sprague waits three more heartbeats and then commands, "Launch!" He continues to watch the chronometer, ticking away the seconds.

J'Kal triggers the release button. From the bay they hear to whoosh of devices being expelled from the launch tubes. J'Kal tracks each device as it speeds to its predetermined location and stops.

"All drones deployed, sir. Raising shields. I sure hope these work, sir."

Around the Hyperion a dense, almost opaque shimmer appears surrounding the craft.

Sprague never takes his eyes off the sensor array.

"Come on, come on. The convoy will be here in less than …"

Four ships fold into space not a thousand klicks from Hyperion.

"Now, J'Kal!"

J'Kal hits a trigger and dozens of harmless plasm bombs light up space around them for klicks, effectively hiding Hyperion and blinding the other four ships. The mercenary ships spin and juke trying to find a target but the expanding balls of multicolored plasm hide everything visible to the eye in the area. But their sensors are not fooled and all four ships turn to target the Hyperion.

J'Kal slams another detonation button and instantly a dozen high energy EMP drones detonate, sending a cascading series of electromagnetic energy pulses blossoming from each device, the waves of energy overlapping each other to engulf the Hyperion and all the surrounding space.

All five ships are caught in the energy surges, causing massive overloads of shipboard systems on the mercenary vessels. The four enemy ships shudder, sputter, go dark and then start spinning and drifting aimlessly.

"Lower the shield, J'Kal!"

The shimmer dissolves and Sprague looks at his control system panels. Everything is still alive and functioning. He lets out a whoop in relief. "Yes! It worked!"

His fingers dance over the sensor array, verifying the mercenary ships are dead in space. "I don't see the Crak Toh!" To the port of the Hyperion another ship materializes. An Identity ping identifies it as the missing ship. J'Kal frantically spins the turret and gets off a frantic shot at the ship to disable it but it folds again, leaving its fleet behind.

"Sorry, Captain, it folded too quickly for me to get a good shot at it. Damn!"

Twenty thousand klicks towards the planet space is suddenly filled with dozens of convoy ships. As each ship completes the transit it immediately heads for the planet as planned.

"Hyperion, this is Goggin Prime. I see you've crippled them. Well done! We have to escort the convoy to the planet, there may be more thieves waiting. Can you deal with those four ships? We'll return as soon as the convoy is safely docked planet side."

"Go ahead, Goggin, we can deal with these bastards. But get back here as soon as you can, we want to pursue that fifth ship."

"Acknowledged, Hyperion. We should be back in less than an hour." With that the Goggin veers off towards the tail of the convoy at high speed.

"J'Kal, do you think you can keep our guests quiet for a little while?"

Four quick precision blasts from the Hyperion's turret and the drive nacelles on the drifting ships are turned to worthless slag. In seconds there are four slightly toasted hulks tumbling aimlessly in space.

J'Kal turns to Sprague with a smug look. "I think that will keep them for a while, sir. I don't think they'll risk firing on us when their systems come back online, assuming they can get them operational. Without drives, they would be sitting ducks in a fire fight."

Sprague smiles broadly and says, "Yes. Nice shooting XO. Now we wait for the Goggin to return before we can go find the Crak Toh on Sewer City."

"Any ideas what to do when we get there?"

"Not a clue, Eva. Not a clue."

*****

Arlo ducks again to avoid being clawed. Krmot is dancing around the small bridge of the Crak Toh, screaming hysterically and swinging mindlessly at everyone and everything in reach. Sparks and small streams of smoke are leaking from several overhead lines. One of the crew is desperately trying to extinguish the fires and not get slashed himself.

"Noooo. Arrgghhh! I'll murder those bastards! I'll crush them under my feet till there is nothing left but eyeballs!" He takes another swipe at Arlo's back, but Arlo's ready for it and dodges. Finally spent, Krmot plops back into his chair, his eyes red and smoldering.

"What happened, Captain?" Arlo asks innocently. It's all he can do to not do a jig of joy himself. "What was all that plasma doing at the target point? Were those our mates?"

Krmot slaps his chair arm and fumes, "You fool, of course they were our ships! And they were adrift in some sort of FTG trap! Those plasma bombs were just for show to keep us from getting a visual on the convoy. I'll bet my last nibbet my ships were disabled by some kind of energy blast, just like the EMP bombs we were going to use!"

Trying to keep Krmot off-guard, Arlo says, "Damn Cap what was that? I folded back as soon as that other ship started firing at us." The bridge crew are watching out the corner of their eyes, wondering if Krmot would space the new Number One for leaving the other ships behind.

Krmot snorts and huffs a few more times, trying to get himself under control. He considers what might have happened if his new First Mate had not folded back right away. He straightens up in his chair and gives Arlo a broad smile.

He waves his hand dismissively at Arlo, "Damn straight you did the right thing, Number One. A half a second more and I would have gave the order myself. I hate to leave our mates behind but there was nothing we could do for them. Well done." He nods his pleasure at Arlo and sits back in his chair.

"Make for Sewer City, Kong. We need to grab what's left of our goods and find another port to make operations on. If I know our mates on those ships, they'll be giving up our hideout to save their own worthless skins. We have to be quick. See to it as soon as we dock."

"Aye, aye, Captain." Arlo plugs in the coordinates and engages the drive. "We'll be back in the landing bay in fifteen."

*****

The Crak Toh settles back into the bay, its hull popping and creaking as the metal cools. The boarding ramp lowers and the crew quickly spill out, heading for the bar.

Arlo lets out a shrill whistle that halts the mad rush down the ramp. "Pass the word. Grab whatever booty you can carry and report back to the Crak Toh. We leave in two hours. We won't wait for stragglers." The crew doesn't like it but they all know it's the only way to stay ahead of the FTG.

Pygee, the only other Snsh onboard the Crak Toh, turns and sidles up to Arlo. He looks around waiting for the rest of the crew to disembark. Satisfied that the two are alone on the ramp, he presses a sharp talon onto Arlo's chest and says just loud enough for their ears, "See here, Kong. What about our mates on those ships we turned tail on?"

"What do you mean, Pygee? Do you want to go back and join them?

Pygee spits on the deck and stares into Arlo's beady eyes. "H'nsn's burning balls no, Number One. I mean what about the loot we all store back there in the bay storage?" He gazes toward the far back of the bay at a line of lockers. "Seems a waste to just leave it here." His evil grin stretches from ear hole to ear hole.

Arlo barks out loud and then leans in closer to the greedy Snsh. "I do believe I see your point, Mr. Pygee. I believe they would want us to make sure it doesn't fall into the Federations' filthy hands. Don't you agree?"

"Aye, sir, I do."

"Then perhaps you should relieve the lockers of those goods and store them onboard the Crak Toh. Just for safety's sake." Arlo raises his own extended talon in warning. "I trust you'll have the good sense to keep this between us, Mr. Pygee. An eighty-twenty split seems proper to me. Eighty for me, of course."

"What?! You greedy dog! I'll not stand for this! It was my idea, you scum sucking…"

Arlo extends his talon further and says, "Yes. And the Cap might like to know that you didn't include him in your idea."

The Snsh snorts and looks around fearfully.

Arlo retracts his talon and says, "I like you, Pygee. Let's make it seventy-thirty and be done with it. Agreed?"

The Snsh grinds his teeth, his face puckering in barely suppressed anger, like he's passing a bag of razor blades. He puffs up on his stubby tail and flips his hood back off his scaly head and is ready to fling a vicious pirate's oath at Arlo when Krmot walks past them and down the ramp, nodding to Arlo as he passes.

Pygee deflates like a popped balloon, settling back on his haunches. He crinkles his snout and smears the mucus running from his nostrils onto the back of his arm, adding another layer to the crust already there.

"Aye, Number One. Agreed." He turns and stomps down the ramp heading for the back of the bay.

Chapter Twenty Two

"A wwwoord, Captainn?"

Woktok steams up to Krmot just as the fuming Snsh smashes a fist onto the crowded bar in the back of the bay. A small cloud of filthy oil mist swirls around them both and slowly settles to the deck. Several crewmen cough and move down to the other end of the bar trying to escape the noxious fumes.

Krmot sneers at the jumble of junk parts, brushing a layer of black dust from the bar. "Not so close, you stinking junkyard." Krmot reaches behind the bar and grabs a tall jar of something mind altering and slams it on the bar surface. He pulls the top off the jar and pours a thick golden-green liquid down his throat. He keeps chugging until the jar is empty then he heaves the jar against the bulkhead, shattering it into a hundred pieces.

"Pleassseee, sir. Thiiss is imporrtantt!"

Krmot reaches behind the bar and drags out another jar, popping the top and taking a big gulp before setting it down on the bar. He wipes his mouth and sighs, his anger dissipating under the influence of the brew. He pushes off the bar and turns to the Clk Dar.

"What do you want, Woktok? I signaled ahead for the rest of our ships to make ready to leave as quickly as possible. The FTG can't be more than an hour behind us. Didn't you get the word?"

"Yyess sirrr. I've notified all mercenary shipsss and crewwss. It wasss not well receeeived, sir, asss I'm sure you willl underrrstand. Twelvvve of the mercenary shiiipss have taken your waaarning and are preparing to leavvve. The ressst have decided to lay lowww here in the Ciittty."

"Let the fools stay, it's no skin off my snout. So what's so important, 'tok?"

"It'ssss your new XO and hisss pettt, sssssir." He extends a segmented arm so that Krmot can see the data chip he's holding.

Krmot lowers his drink quickly and steps towards Woktok, waving the fumes to the side and glancing at the chip. He grabs the chip and says, "What about them, gearhead?"

"That is a report of their DDNA samplesss, sssir. The onesss I take when crewww sign on." The Clk Dar's 'head' spins slowly and wobbles on its rickety torso, almost toppling the body. Krmot grabs the creature and pops its head with a wham! Woktok seems to settle again, some kind of dark green liquid squirting from the bottom, leaving a small puddle. Woktok swivels his head down and sees the puddle. "Oh, myyyy. That'sss not gooddd."

Krmot loses his patience and pops Woktok's head again. "Spit it out or there's going to be a lot more of you spread around the bay! What does this report say about their DNA samples?"

"They are not whatttt they say they are, sssir. They have been modified somehow. Kong's DNA hasss the markers forrr a much smaller reptile, probbabbly from a planet called Eeeearthh. Hisss pett appears to have been a humannnn male."

"Human?"

"Yesss, ssir. Huuman."

Krmot rubs his temples in concentration. "A human and a lizard. Why does that raise alarms in my mind?" He grabs his mug and raises it to his lips. His eyes open wide as his mind finally provides the faces it's looking for. He slowly lowers the mug, his hand trembling slightly. "Arlo the Devastator..." he whispers. "Arlo the Devastator and Jake Jaspers, his partner. Of course!"

"Arlo the Devvvv…, eekkk!" Woktok yelps.

Krmot slams the mug on Woktok's spinning head, grinding it to a stop.

"Quiet, you fool! We don't want them to know that we know! Stop your damn clanking and spitting and let me think for a minute."

His mind races back to the day the two reported to him. "Didn't you scan them for Federation implants?"

"Yessss, wee did. They don'ttt have anyyy."

"They must have ripped them out knowing we'd check for them before taking them on as crew. Damn!"

Woktok looks around at the chaos around them and says, "Sshouln't we be geetingg ready to leecave, ssir?"

"We'll leave when I say so! Find Crow and send him to me. Then find B'inDere and D'unDat and have them take their ships out to the edge of the system and scout for any FTG ships. We'll have plenty of time to make it out before they can get here. Go!"

Woktok spins around twice and speeds off in a cloud of black smoke towards the Crak Toh.

Seething inside, Krmot nurses his drink trying to figure out what to do with this revelation. FTG infiltrators on his crew! How did they know? Did he have a mole in his crew? Did someone sell them out?

"You wanted to see me, Cap?"

Krmot turns to Crow with an evil smile on his face. "I think I know how our ships were ambushed, Crow. We have us some traitors in the crew! It's all on this report." He tossed the data chip onto the bar.

Crow scowls and picks up the data chip. "What does it say, Cap? Who are they?"

Krmot grabs two more jugs from behind the bar and passes one to Crow. "A couple of friends of yours." He tells Crow about Woktok's discovery.

"H'nsn's flamin' nads! Arlo the Devastator? How is that possible?" Crow gasps.

"The Clk Dar says they've been bio-modified somehow. That means the Feds must suspect G'radian has been operating out of Sewer City. They must have sent these scabs to infiltrate and then sell us out! And it almost worked!"

"So that's how our ships were waylaid!" Crow crushed the jar, mangling it and then sending it crashing against the bulkhead. "I KNEW those two were trouble, Cap! I knew there was something strange about them showing up just before we left on that run."

Krmot nods and lies, "So did I, mate, so did I. I couldn't say anything 'till I knew for sure. I always wanted you as my new First Mate, Crow. I was shocked when your pet lost! What could I do in front of the crew?"

Crow raises his eyebrows a bit in barely concealed disbelief, but says, "Thank you, Captain." He chews his lower lip and says, "I think I know how to deal with these two scumbags, sir. What do you say to another fight? They won't know we're onto them. Do we have time? We could arrange for a little surprise for them after my pet slices the skin off that pink freak."

Krmot rubs his scaly chin, revenge eating into his brew addled brain. He knows he should just have Crow blast Kong right where he is and then take care of his pet but his anger at losing the ships and the booty are overriding his common sense. If he had any, that is.

He finally slams his fist on the bar and barks, "We'll make time, damn their hides! The scout ships will give us plenty of warning." He looks around the bay and points to some crewman standing around. "Grab those goons and set up the fighting ring. Then pass the word about the fight. I'll leave it to you to arrange for the surprise."

Crow grins from ear to ear. "I'll see to it, Captain." He turns and strides over to the small group of pirates, eager to get his revenge started.

A hooded figure at the end of the bar lowers his mug, pulls his cover tighter around his shoulders and moves silently out into the corridor.

****

Arlo has been watching the bay from the top of ramp, taking in the seeming chaos while he desperately tries to come up with an idea to save himself, Jake and Kasha. When Woktok speeds off and Crow rushes to Krmot's side, his hackles literally start to rise. Something is definitely up. And since Krmot is not including Arlo in it, it can't be good.

When Crow moves off Arlo turns and walks quickly up the ramp to find Jake. He moves as fast as he can through the converted freighter's narrow corridors towards their cramped quarters. Arlo keys the portal, glances around to see if he was followed and steps inside.

Jake is laying down on the floor, the only way he can stretch out to his full height. His toes have punctured the bulkhead in a dozen places. He ears are mushed down around his head. When Arlo pops in, he sits up, bending his head low to clear the ceiling. "What's up? You look like you just saw a Marphka in heat."

Arlo says, "Worse. I think Krmot and Crow are onto us. I saw Krmot huddled with that bundle of nuts and bolts, Woktok, looking up at me without trying to look up at me. The Captain seemed real peeved about something. Then Woktok took off in a cloud of smoke. Crow showed up a few seconds later and huddled with Krmot like two spies in a bad movie. We need to get Kasha right now and get off this tub." He turns and keys the portal, stepping through without looking back.

Jake bends lower to miss banging his head on the portal. He pushes through the opening and steps smack into a circle of pirates, all with their blasters drawn. Arlo is standing with his snout an inch from Crow's ugly face, his weapons on the floor.

Arlo is screaming at the top of voice, "What the hell are you doing, you low life scum…" He stops abruptly when Crow shoves his blaster into Arlo's side.

Crow snarls and says, "It means the ruse is up you Federation filth." He shoves the blaster deeper into Arlo's ribs and growls, "We know you're Arlo the Devastator." He points his chin at Jake and says, "And that's your lackey, Jake Jasper."

In my mind I snarl, "You've got to be kidding. Lackey?" I start to rise and get a couple of blasters shoved in my haunches. Not cool.

"Sit, Boo Boo," pings back Arlo in my mind. "Cowboy up here or we're toast."

"Has booze curdled your mind, Crow? Do we look like a scummy little Earth lizard and a puny human? Have you seen those guys? They're pathetic. I could squash Arlo with one toenail." Arlo raises an extended talon and plants it on Crow's nose and then points it to me. "Does my pet look like a cursed FTG human puke? How the hell could we be them?!"

Crow slowly raises a hand, the data chip in his palm. "This is how, numb nuts. Woktok had your DNA samples analyzed. You're an Earth lizard and that…" he eyes me with a fierce squint, "…is Jake Jasper, a human. We know you've be bio-modified and had your implants removed."

He puts the data chip in a pocket and continues, "Clever plan, I admit. You must have found out that G'radian was using Sewer City for a base. Too bad for you that G'radian turned yellow and took off. You must have got here just in time for Krmot to take over the operations. Bad luck for you."

"I think our goose is cooked, Arlo," I thought. "We need to stall for time, buddy."

"Yeah. Play it cool for now. Let's see if we can make a break for it outside."

Crow holsters his blaster and steps back. "OK, mates. Get these two outside. We have a little surprise for them."

Hands held as high as we can in the corridor we start a bizarre parade towards the loading ramp. This does not bode well for the good guys. "Arlo, any brilliant ideas, buddy. I don't want to die as big fat pink bunny."

"Quiet, Jake. I'm trying to contact Kasha. Get ready to boogey once we're outside."

Oh, right. He might be able to use his telepathic link to tell Kasha what's going on.

As they march us out of the ship's bay portal to the ramp my heart sinks. I expected the landing area to be empty, but it's just the opposite. It's packed with at least a hundred mercenaries, all facing us, some their weapons drawn. Crap.

Arlo pings me. "OK. Keep calm, Jake. Looks like we're not going to make a run for it here."

"No shit, Sherlock," I retort.

In the center of the launching bay they've set up another fighting arena. The Crak Toh's crew aren't the only pirates though, there are enough mercs to crew half a dozen fighters. Most of them are gathering around the buzzing ring of blaster lines and more are coming in from the bay's corridor.

Arlo pings me again. "Krmot is using us to rally more mercenaries, Jake. This is bad. Even if we make it out of this fight, we can't just grab a ship and skip out. They will fry us before we got out of the system."

He's right, damn it! Krmot is stirring up a fresh batch of scurvy pirates fast. "Sweet Jezebel, buddy, we're so screwed!" I can see Woktok taking bets on the far side of the ring. I wonder who our opponent will be this time.

"Oh, shit, Jake. I just contacted Kasha and ..."

I already know what he's going to say. I can see Kasha coming down the ramp. She's obviously trying to fight Crow, jerking down the ramp and struggling to keep her balance. "I can see her, partner. This is going from crappy to really, really not nice very quickly."

"I'm going to tell her stop fighting so hard, we don't want Crow to suspect that we know each other."

Kasha is still stiff walking towards us but looks less like a jerking marionette. Good, maybe Crow won't notice the change.

Arlo and I are marched up to the side of the ring, the mercs give us a wide berth. These guys must not have livers because they're already three sheets to wind, even though some of them just got off the Crak Toh. On the other hand they probably never stop drinking. Pirate's Code of Conduct Rule number twelve. Right after number eleven; never, ever shower.

Crow grabs Kasha by the elbow as she steps up next to us. "I'm going to break you to the control, bitch, if it's the last thing I do." He thumbs a button on his slave control. Kasha's eyes roll back in her head and she cries out in agony. Crow holds the button for several seconds, Kasha screaming the whole time.

He releases the stud and Kasha's howl trails away to heart rending sobs.

Arlo's ping is cold as ice. "If I get a chance, I'm going to take great joy in showing this bastard his own entrails."

"Fine. Then I get to hurt him, partner."

Someone has found a crate for Krmot to stand on. He waves his hands for quiet. The raucous mob slowly quiets enough for him to be heard.

"Enough, now! Can it!" He looks around at the crowd, grinning like Silvester with Tweety's butt hanging out of his mouth. "This isn't just another pet fight, my mates! I've found out how our poor mates were ambushed!"

Next to the ramp Woktok shudders, sputters and spews oily steam out the top of his head, infuriated that the captain is taking credit for his discovery. Murmurs of surprise start percolating around the crowd, tempers rising quickly.

Before the Clk Dar can spout out his protest, Krmot continues, "That's right, mates. They were ambushed. Someone ratted us out. Someone in our own crew!" He waves his hands to encircle Arlo and me. "And the traitors are right here!"

It's suddenly eerily quiet in the launch bay. All heads and eyes focus on us. Suddenly blasters, swords and other sharp thingies are out and the crowd starts to surge around the ring.

Krmot realizes he's about to lose control so he brings his blaster up and fires it towards the crates at the back of the bay. There's a scream from behind the crates and poor Pygee stumbles forward, his arms full of booty. He takes a few steps and falls forward onto his charred face. Krmot cringes and then straightens back up before anyone notices that it was a mistake.

It has the effect of stopping the mob though. Everyone glances at the smoldering heap by the crates and then back to Krmot. Instantly all weapons are sheathed and they step back from the ring.

Krmot shakes off his shock at blasting poor Pygee and growls, "That's what happens to anyone looking to make off with our poor mates loot." He bends down to Crow and whispers, "Send one our mates to get that loot and stash it in your new stateroom. Crow nods.

He waves his gun in a small circle and then holsters it. "So. Do you know who we have here, mates?" He points to Arlo and then me. "None other than the infamous Arlo the Devastator and his partner, Jake Jasper."

There's a collective gasp and the whole mob takes a choreographed half step back. A few heartbeats of silence. Again like a bad musical troupe the mob steps forward again, their faces suddenly masks of fury.

Uh. This is not good.

Krmot whips his gun out and fires a blast over the Crak Toh, sending molten bulkhead metal flying over the mob.

"Stop! We want them to pay for betraying our mates and losing the booty that they've taken from us. Right? What do you say to a Death Match, my brothers and sisters? These two traitors against Crow's pet and Augie's pet? Want a little payback? Want to see a little blood and guts before we go find another base? Want to watch these two get sliced into little pieces?"

The mob mulls it over for a moment and then settles back on their heels again. Then a chant starts up… "Death Match! Death Match! Death Match…" The chant gets louder and louder, reverberating in the bay like a Roman gladiator movie.

Crow shoves Arlo and me into the ring and then turns to a thick limbed Gruenite standing in the crowd. "Augie! Get your pet and get ring side."

The burly pirate nods and races into the Crak Toh.

"This is not good, Jake," Arlo complains in my mind. "But Kasha says she'll do everything she can to help us if she gets the chance."

"That's something, buddy, but I think we're going to need a serious miracle this time. Take a look at Augie's pets."

Lumbering down the ramp behind Augie is a pair of four foot tall Nars, jaws jutting from their small heads, snapping like a crocodiles on speed. Nars are bio-tank grown battle fodder and banned throughout the civilized galaxies. Their bodies resemble hyenas. Their squat, massively muscled body are covered with scales instead of hair. Their misshapen heads are mostly fang filled mouth, the eyes are barely visible on top, like a crocs except they are perched at the toothy end of the head. They are mindless killers, hard to break to the collar. But once they are 'tamed' they fight until they have killed or their owners uses the controller to knock them out.

"Oh, jeez," pings Arlo. He hesitates and then says, "Kasha just told me that Augie's pets are the most vicious pets she has ever fought. Most of her scars came from Crow making her fight them for the crew's pleasure."

"Great. We're about to enter a ring lined with deadly blaster rays, fight a couple of tanks with sharp teeth and talons and a super ninja woman who we can't fight. The Universe sucks, buddy. It truly does."

"Well it could be worse, buddy. At least we know Kasha won't try to kill us."

"Yeah, but as soon as Crow realizes that he'll probably kill Kasha."

"Kasha has already thought of that. She wants you to fight her and I'll take on the mini-gators. I think I can keep them at bay if I can keep them in a corner. You two put up a fight until the three of us can turn on the Nars and take them out. Then you slice a post and hope that we can cut our way through the crowd and make a run for the corridor."

"Oh sure. I get the female buzz saw and you get a couple of cute little gremlins. That sounds fair."

Before Arlo can kick my whinny butt Crow shouts, "Put them into the ring, mates! Let's watch some blood flow!"

The crowd parts. Arlo and I are shoved into the twenty foot square match ring and the beams reenergized. We rush to opposite sides, each taking a corner and then turn to face our opponents. Arlo has extended his talons to full length. I dig my hooks into the decking to anchor me so I can swing better. My talons are slowly sliding in and out, my body sensing that danger is near. I can feel my heart rate rising as the fight response kicks in.

Arlo pings me softly in my heated noggin'. "You OK, Jake? You've got that nasty 'I want to kill something' look on your face! Remember, Kasha is on our side."

OK. Let's slow things down here. I try to slow my breathing and let my racing heart calm itself. I ping back, "Yeah. Yeah. I'm trying. Just tell her to try not to slice and dice anything important, OK? Are you sure you can handle those two without me?"

"We're about to find out, Jake. Good luck."

Kasha and the Nars step up to the ring, jerking like puppets on a string, their masters controlling their movements. Crow and Augie have taken a front row position, the space around them cleared of mercs so that they can use their controllers.

Krmot is still on his crate, ready to watch the fight from there. His voice booms over the crowd. "Are you ready to watch these Federation scumbags get what's coming to them?"

The crowd burst into cheers. "Death Match! Death Match!"

The section of the ring in front of Augie and Crow fizzles and dies. Kasha and the Nars step into the ring and the plasma flares back to life. Or death. Depending on how you look at.

Arlo bellows in his best John Wayne, "Come and get some, Pilgrim!"

Arlo quickly steps in front of the Nars and tries to behead them both with a massive swipe of his claws. To evade the strike both Nars dive to the left. Arlo drives them into the corner, constantly swinging his arms and front legs while trying to evade those jaws.

I don't have time to admire his fighting prowess though, Kasha has let out an agonizing scream and leaped into the air with both swords aimed at my head. Methinks planting my feet was a very, very stupid thing to do.

Before I can rip my feet away from the decking Kasha brings both swords down in a flying arc aimed to my left. I bend my upper torso wildly bringing both claws up to defend. I catch her swords in my left talons and back hand her across the ring, head over heels. She manages to hold onto her weapons but I can see I've hurt her. She's bent to her side, favoring her ribs. She glares at me and gets wobbly back onto her feet.

I glance to my right hoping to see if my buddy is still alive. He's still got the Nars backed into the corner and swinging but he's bleeding from a gash on his back and is missing a piece of his tail. Damn!

"Stay with me, Arlo! We've got to get into position to…AARRRGGGHHH!" A stab of searing pain lances my head. I instinctively swing out with my paw and connect with Kasha, sending her flying back to the other side of the ring again.

Hot blood in pouring down the left side of my head. I reach up to where my cute bunny ear used to be and look down. The pink leathery pulp is twitching at my feet. She cut my damn ear off!

The pain is excruciating, she cut it all the way down to the skull this time! A scream escapes from my open maw and all my teeth have popped down, ready to rip and shred whatever I can find. I step forward, a red haze filling my vision. All I can think of is killing something.

"Jake! Jake! Catch!" yells someone in my mind. I feel something coming from my right and I extend my claws to grab whatever it is. It's a Nar with one leg missing, flying jaws over claws right at me. My talons extend fully and I skewer the animal like bloody bratwurst on a pitch fork. I shove it into my mouth, clamping on its scaly head and before I can stop myself I rip the head from the body.

The silence is stunning. I slowly look around the crowd of mercenaries, the Nar's crushed head dripping green, clotted blood down my face, chin and chest. A low, rumbling growl escapes my throat. I raise my head and spit the mangled head into the mass of wide eyed mercenaries on the other side of the beams. The head smashes into the ones in front, splattering blood, bones and teeth everywhere.

A high pitched animal scream is suddenly cut off to my right. It snaps me back to reality and I look for my buddy, hoping it's not his scream I heard.

Arlo is standing on his rear legs, balancing on his stubby tail. In his hands and front legs he is holding the back half of the other Nar. The front half is flopping madly on the outside of the ring. He's used the plasma beam to cut the animal in two.

The left side of his face is a mess, the Nar must have caught him in its jaws. Arlo's front left arm is gushing blood where the hand used to be.

Kasha, Arlo and I look at each other and the crowd. We slowly walk, Kasha in front, towards the ring side where Crow and Augie are standing, dumbfounded. Augie is still pressing studs on his controller, not fully aware that his pets are far from being able to respond. He looks down at his controller and then to the bloody parts of his animals strewn around the ring. His face turns a painful red and lets out a horrible yell. "Noooooo!"

Kasha starts screaming in pain. Crow is holding down a stud on his controller, his face contorted with fury. "Kill them or I'll fry every nerve in your body, bitch! Fight!"

Kasha continues to scream but walks slowly and steadily towards Crow, pain wracking her body. Arlo and I are on either side of her now.

Crow steps back from the ring, out of our reach, but continuing to press studs on Kasha's controller on his wrist.

Suddenly a cloaked figure pushes through the crowd next to Crow. A sizzling bright green sword slashes down to strike Crow's outstretched arm. The blade slams into the controller and without stopping continues through his arm, severing it. Half of the controller and the end of Crow's arm fall to the deck. Kasha's screams stop.

"Now, Jake, now!" screams Arlo out loud.

I sling the body of the Nar still skewered on my paw at the ring post to our left. It crashes into the post and a snaps it at the base. The beam in front of us disappears in an instant. Kasha takes two steps forward and swings her right sword. The singing sword cleanly decapitates Crow just above the shoulders. Without hesitating she swings her left sword back and cuts Augie in half, severing him at heart level. Both bodies waver for an instant and then thud to the deck. Kasha slumps next to them, blood pouring from the wound in her side.

Before anyone can take another breath the roar of a ship echoes in the crowded bay. The ship careens into the bay, headed right for our bloody party. Mercenaries scatter madly in all directions.

His hood pulled back, the man shouts at us. "Hurry! Clear a path for us to the ship!"

Arlo and I ram through the thinning crowd, swinging our claws and talons at any pirate stupid enough to get in our way.

The stranger picks up Kasha and slings her over his shoulder and makes a mad dash for the ship, slicing through any merc unfortunate enough to be too close to his sizzling blade.

The mystery ship's bay door is open the ramp slamming onto the decking. Under the nose of the ship a gun turret spins and opens fire, sending more mercs running for cover and vaporizing any that are too slow.

Blaster fire crisscrosses on each side of us as we run up the ramp. "Get that ramp up," screams the pilot over the ship's intercom.

I dive into the bay and roll to the side. Arlo jumps in right behind me and turns to grab our rescuer and Kasha just as the ship starts to rises, dragging the ramp along the deck.

The man flips Kasha from his shoulder into my arms just as a blaster bolt strikes him squarely in the back. He falls forward into the ship's open maw. Arlo slams the door stud and the portal closes instantly, snapping the remaining section of the ramp outside the hull.

I can feel the ship turning wildly about and heading away from Sewer City. Seconds later a young man runs into the bay. His eyes go wide when he sees the hooded man lying face down on the deck, a shallow dark red pit still smoldering in his back.

"Father!" he cries and kneels down. I don't know how but the man rolls over onto his back and opens his eyes. He cringes in pain but says, "Get us out of the system now, son, they will be coming for us!"

The young man seems to waver but says, "Yes, father." He rises and looks at our motley group and points to our right. "Get father and the wounded to the sick bay, there is an emergency medical system there. Get Father out of his armor and onto the med table and see to your own wounds. As quickly as you can I'll need one of you in the cockpit. Father can explain while you're there. Hurry, we haven't much time!"

He was gone before I could protest. "Arlo, can you lift this man?" I say, looking at his stubby limb, blood oozing around the stub where his hand had been. "I've got Kasha."

Arlo uses his front legs and other arm to flip the man up and across his back. "Yeah, I've got him. Let's go."

We limp through the corridor and straight into the small med compartment. There is only one tiny med bunk. Laying Kasha on the bed automatically activates the system. A probe on a thin arm extends down from the wall and starts scanning her body from head to toe. A small vid screen comes to life displaying medical information which is all geek to me. Manipulators drop from the overhead and start cutting Kasha's uniform away from her wounds.

A tinny voice says, "Patient has several severe lacerations, multiple contusions and three broken ribs. Injuries are non-life threatening at this point."

"Doc, emergency repairs first. Get the patient stable, we'll deal with her other problems later."

"Acknowledged."

"We need get Kasha's wound staunched before she bleeds out. Here, you run the doc and I'll get this guy out of his armor or whatever. I can't believe he's still alive!"

Arlo nods and sets the man on the lone stool in the corner. We trade places and I start stripping the man's upper clothing. Sure enough he has some kind of powered armor under his cloak and tunic. Where the blaster hit the armor is a fist sized crater with blood trickling through. It looks like the blast made it through the armor but I can't tell how far. It takes me a few minutes to figure out how to find and unfasten the clasps. I begin to peel the wrap around armor from his body. As I lift it away from his back he jerks back to consciousness with a loud cry of pain.

"Stay still! We'll get you on the med table in a minute, but you need to stay still so you don't make it worse."

The man moans and looks at me. "Thank you. Are we away? Did Bolton get us out of the system yet?"

"Bolton. Is he the pilot?"

"Yes. He's my son." His eyes go in and out of focus and then he coughs up some blood. "I'm Ryan G'radian."

You could have pushed me over with a feather. I turn to Arlo to see if he heard. He did.

"You're G'radian?" barked Arlo. "Aren't you supposed to be the leader of those mercs that tried to fry our asses back there?"

Kasha is sitting up on the bed, a fresh bandage around her ribs. She looks at G'radian suspiciously. "He was. I heard through the net that he killed one of the pirates and then ran."

G'radian starts to say something, coughs up some more blood and passes out into my arms.

"We'll figure this out later. Kasha, move over to the portal while Arlo and I get G'radian onto the table."

Kasha moves gingerly into the corridor and we get G'radian on his stomach on the table.

The med doc comes to life again and starts scanning.

"Life signs are fluctuating. Patient has sustained critical injuries to his internal organs. Attempting to stabilize." More bleeps, pings and whirrs and then, "Patient will not survive without access to a full med unit and healing tank."

Arlo curses, "Damn! This is messed up! Why the hell did G'radian come back for us if he's the leader of those pirates? They could have been half way across the Galaxy by now, free and clear."

"Maybe his son can tell us." I look at Kasha and say, "Can you co-pilot this ship? Arlo and I can stay with G'radian. I might be able to help with weapons but I'm too big to sit second chair in a ship like this."

Kasha stands and says, "Yes, I can assist the pilot. Do something for me first?" She pulls the collar out from her neck. "It's disabled but I can't remove it by myself."

"With pleasure." I extend my claws and put one on each side of her neck, under the collar. I carefully pull outward until the collar snaps in two, falling to the deck. There are circles of tiny scars and pits around her neck where the collar sat.

Kasha pokes at the collar with a foot, frowning. "I will not rest until slavery is banned in this sector. No one should live like that." She kicks the loathsome device to a corner and turns to portal. "I'll see what I can do for Bolton." She sprints out of the lab and into the corridor.

Arlo is scanning the med status vid and shaking his head. "It doesn't look good for G'radian. If we don't get him to a full med facility soon he won't make it."

"You stay with him, Arlo. You might want to strap him down in case things go sour."

"In case?" he chuckles. "You mean when, right?"

I smile and step out into the corridor, heading for the bridge. I wonder what the hell we can do when Krmot finds us, which of course he will. It's only a matter of …

A giant fist slams the ship, knocking me against the wall. OK. I guess it's now.

Chapter Twenty Three

Krmot is screaming at the chaos in the bay. Pirates are running around in a panic, some firing at the receding freighter ship, their small arms doing no real damage to the ship.

"Stop! Stop firing, you idiots, you can't hurt that ship! Stop!" he screams. He jumps up and down frantically, the crate wobbling wildly. "Captains! Captains! Here! Quickly mates or they'll get away!" He fires over the heads of the mob striking an outer bulkhead. The blast sends shrapnel raining down on some of the unlucky mercs.

He spies several merc captains and waves for them frantically. "Jubal, Klick, Qui! All captains, get over here."

A dozen mercs rush to Krmot, some not looking all that pleased at being ordered around by the little Snsh.

"Who the hell are you to…"

Krmot seizes the moment before it gets away. "Enough! We can tally up the damages later. We need to organize right now and go after that ship before it leaves the system. I want G'radian and those Federation bastards dead! Don't you?"

Several of the mercs nod vigorously. A huge Grockna in the front yells, "That's right! I want blood for blood, Krmot."

Thanking his lucky stars for Jubal's support he says, "All captains get to your ships. I'll contact my scouts. They'll be able to spot that ship before it can leave the system. Then we'll blast the scum into dark space. A thousand credits to the ship that destroys that freighter!"

"Aye, Captain Krmot!" yells Jubal, his big fist raised in salute. Jubal turns to the other captains and says, "Well? Which one of you puss-faced pirates is going to be buying the first round tonight?"

The crowd at Krmot's feet turns as one, some running to ships squatting next to the Crak Toh, other full tilt out into the corridor to other landing bays. They are all yelling at the top of their lungs for their crews to scramble to their ships.

Krmot chuckles smugly to himself. "You idiots will be fighting for months about who actually destroys the ship. I'll never have to give that reward to anyone!"

He steps down from the crate and runs for the Crak Toh. Woktok is practically vibrating in place, spewing a cloud of noxious fumes all around the ramp entrance. 'Ssship is readddy to launch, Cccaptain, mostttt the crrrew are onbbboard. Do weee wait for rrrrrest?"

Krmot doesn't even hesitate at the portal. "No! Raise the ramp now. Get to your stations!" He yells into the intercom, "Trzz, launch now. Contact B'inDere and get a report on that ship!"

Pirate ships start to form up behind the Crak Toh as it streaks for the edge of the system.

Krmot straps into his chair and glances at the sensor array. There are at least ten ships following in loose formation. Damn. He won't be able to hang back this time, the mercs would see it as blatant cowardice.

Krmot thumbs his com and says, "B'inDere, have you spotted that ship yet?"

"Aye, Captain! I've sent you her current heading and speed. You will get to it faster than I can, do you want me to try to intercept?"

"No! I don't want them to know you've spotted them. Stay there and notify us if they change course."

"Yes, Captain."

"I have them on sensors now, Captain," says his weapons officer triumphantly. "We're close enough for the long range beam cannon. Can I fire?"

"Hell yes, you fool, fire! If we nail her that bounty is ours to keep!"

A stream of pure energy erupts from on the side wing of the Crak Toh. The forward screen shows the beam, now at its extreme range for damage, strike the fleeing craft on the port side. The ship tumbles for a few seconds and then stabilizes and makes an abrupt course change just as a half dozen other beams pass by harmlessly. The Crak Toh was not the only ship that took a chance on a long range strike. The freighter is venting plasma and it's slowing.

The pirate fleet is gaining quickly on the trader ship.

"We have them now, mates."

Trzz turns to Krmot and says, "Shame we have to blast 'em, Captain. Those two Feds might be worth a fortune in ransom."

The realization hits Krmot like a brick. "Damn my stupid brain," he thinks. "Why didn't I think of that?"

He lies, "I was just wondering about that myself, Trzz. Good to see you're alert. Put me on fleet com. Quickly!"

"Mates, hold fire. Hold fire!"

"Why, Captain?" says Jubal over the comm. "We have them now, let's end this!"

"I have a better solution, Jubal. Since my strike damaged them, they can't escape us. I say we capture the ship, grab them all. G'radian and his brat we give a special one way trip out an air lock. We auction off Crow's pet and we ransom the Feds. They'll be worth a fortune! What say you, mates?"

After barely a moment's hesitation the intercom is filled with greedy mercenaries yelling their approval.

Jubal's voice comes in last. "I believe we are agreed, Captain. We'll leave you the honor of boarding and taking the prisoners."

Krmot was just about to suggest Jubal take that honor but he was too late. Damn! "Thanks, Jubal, I owe you one."

Chapter Twenty Four

"Bolton, what's happening?" I yell, trying to get my feet under me again. The ship is spinning slowly like a careening car on black ice. "Somebody talk to me!" I dig into the decking to regain my balance as I make the last turn to the bridge. I'm just in time to see Kasha strapping into the co-pilots chair. There's not enough room for me to join them so I brace myself against the bulkhead and try to peer through to the video screens.

Bolton looks back at me with a confused look. "They've only hit us once, but it was a lucky long range hit. It hit one of our engine nacelles and the aft stabilizers. This is a modified freighter, not a fighter. It's built for cargo and speed with minimal offense and defense. We only have two cannons forward. I'm trying to correct our spin with auxiliary systems but even if I do I'm not sure I can do much more than basic maneuvering. The main is probably only good for a limited fold." He looks back forward and continues, "I don't understand why they haven't finished us. They are well within range now."

Kasha is scanning the sensors and video screens. She says, "I wondered about that too. They've all stopped about ten thousand klicks away. Wait. It looks like the Crak Toh is moving towards us now."

Bolton keys the intercom and says, "How is my father? Is he still alive?"

Arlo's voice is low and concerned. "He's alive but the med unit says he's critical and failing. The armor didn't stop all of the blast. I'm sorry."

Bolton clinches a fist and pounds the console in anguish. "No. Hold on, Father! Hold on!" His hands fly over the console trying to bring power back to our crippled ship.

I reach in a put a paw on his shoulder. "I'm sorry, Bolton. You risked your lives to rescue us…"

The inter ship intercom crackles to life. It's Krmot. His hissing rasping voice is laced with menace. "G'radian! You cowardly scum. We know your ship is disabled. Stand by to be boarded. Don't do anything stupid and we might let your son and his new friends live."

Kasha says, "Crak Toh is coming in close to starboard. The rest of his fleet is standing off at five thousand klicks." She glances back to me and then to Bolton. "You know he's lying, right? Those cowards are going to grab Arlo, Jake and Me for pets or hostages and then blow this ship to pieces with you and your father onboard. Mercenaries don't have any code of honor no matter what you've heard."

Bolton must have had success bringing some systems back to life, because the ship slowly stops spinning, the pirate fleet becoming visible in our starboard vid screen. The Crak Toh is maneuvering closer now that we've stopped rotating. It's less than a klick away and slowly closing the gap.

Bolton keys the ship's intercom and says, "Arlo. We have to decide what to do right now, before Krmot can energize his hull grips and board us." He looks at Kasha and me and continues, "I've managed to get the impulse engines and the starboard cannon back on line but we've vented a lot of fuel. The main engine might make two or three folds, but they would track us easily and just jump behind us. Then the most we can hope for is to take Krmot and maybe a few more of those fighters out before they blast us to stardust."

We all know what has to be done. None of us are willing to become slaves for these bastards. We'll go out with guns blazing.

I look at Kasha and Bolton and nod. "You know what to do, Bolton. Kasha can incinerate that bastard's ship and then start our last hoorah."

I raise my voice to make sure Arlo hears me and say, "I love you, buddy. It's been a real …"

Over the intercom Arlo's voice breaks in, "Can it, Jake. Bolton! G'radian says to execute the Omega maneuver! Do it now!"

What the hell? "Arlo! Didn't you hear…"

Space around our ship twists and folds like taffy as Bolton punches the main engines to life. The stars snap back into focus, but my stomach continues to flip and I just manage to step to the right in the corridor before I toss my cookies in a molten munchies arch.

Kasha is screaming, "Hard to starboard, Bolton, engage main engines now!"

"I'm doing the best I can!" shouts Bolton. Half of the bridge console lights flicker then go dark, the ship shuddering beneath our feet. A second later the ship shudders again, coming back to life. Bolton frantically jabs a few buttons. "Kasha, get ready to target anyone following us, I'm going to emergency dump the cargo hold."

From the stern of the ship there's a sound like a giant garbage truck farting and the ship is shoved forward a hundred meters. The ship cartwheels slowly, rocking back and forth a couple of times before Bolton can get it under control.

All around us there are cargo crates, straps and other small debris drifting, tumbling and bouncing into each other.

"Ships to port, Bolton!" yells Kasha. I can feel our gun mounts phuff, phuff, phuffing away as Kasha targets and fires on the ships folding in all around us. Jesus, she's good! She's hit two ships in the blink of a pink eye and that's with the Tau still rocking like a rodeo bull with a spiked flank strap.

Tau rocks to starboard, one of the merc's making a glancing hit! I don't think we can take a lot more hits, glancing or otherwise. But it looks like the merc's are nailing the crates a lot more than us. Of course! The crates are screwing with their targeting systems!

Bolton puts us into another spiral burst and suddenly we're through the debris field with half a dozen ships swinging towards us.

"Hold on! Last transit to the Omega rendezvous point!" yells Bolton. The space around us twists weirdly again. Crap, another fold so soon?

My guts twist again as space unfolds itself around us. There's nothing left in my stomach to hurl, but I still heave a few times more.

"That's it! The main engine is off line. We can't fold!" He scans the console and slams the console panel. "Impulse fuel is almost spent, hang on!"

The ship jumps forward like a rodeo bull. I pull myself back to the bridge portal just in time to see a ship flash by from our port quarter, less than a hundred meters away. The Crak Toh! I can see its gun turrets starting to swivel towards us, firing wildly.

Bolton puts us through gut wrenching evasive maneuvers trying to stay out of the direct line of fire. I can't believe we're still in one piece! Kasha is firing back, trying to target the Crak Toh, but it's easily maneuvering out of her line of fire.

Several concussions hit us in quick succession, not heavy but enough to rattle the ship from stem to stern. I can hear G'radian screaming in pain on the med table.

Kasha yells, "The rest of the mercs have folded in. They're maneuvering to surround us. We can't take too many more hits, Bolton, the shields are almost gone!" She points to a vid screen. "Torpedos astern! Evasive, evasive!"

I glance at the aft video screen. There are a dozen dots approaching rapidly. Bolton is not going to be able to evade all of those. This is it.

Suddenly, a dozen brilliant streaks of red plasma beams streak from somewhere above and behind us! Each of the dots disappear in a brilliant ball of plasma. More angry red beams streak by our bridge, flying from above and below our ship.

Kasha yells again, this time with joy. "Yes! Yes! Yes!"

"What, Kasha? What the hell is happening?" I gasp. All the vid screens are suddenly quiet, no flashing beams or explosions. "How the hell did we do that?"

Bolton turns to me but points to the sensors. "It's not us! Krmot's fleet was attacked by FTG ships! They've disabled the pirate fleet! Every one of his ships is either destroyed or dead in space!"

The ship's intercom crackles to life. "Stand down, Un-Jun freighter! This is Lieutenant Doar of the FTG Battle Ship 'H.P. Oliver'. Do not move or activate any weapons. We have you targeted as well." An FTG fighter spins on its nose as it swings to face the front of our freighter. "Mr. Jasper! Mr. Arlo! Respond!"

Kasha keys the inter-ship comm and motions for me to speak.

It takes me a second for my brain to restart. "Uh… this is Jake Jasper. Arlo is in the med bay with a wounded man who needs immediate medical attention. This freighter cannot transit. Can you assist?"

"What is your pet name for Lieutenant Tillet? You have three seconds to respond."

Password protection? "Pixie! It's Pixie!"

There is a brief pause and then the intercom sparks back to life. "OK. That matches our intel, Mr. Jasper." I hear the start of a chuckle just before he keys his mic. Then he's back, "Sorry, Mr. Jasper, but we had almost no time to prepare for this and we needed to make sure we had the right ship and passengers."

There is another short pause. "I've requested a med ship be dispatched immediately. ETA is five minutes. Oliver is currently engaged and cannot respond herself. Make your wounded ready and prepare to transfer everyone when the med ship arrives. Excuse me now. I need to deal with these mercenaries. I will see you on the Oliver."

Doar's ship spins on its axis and moves to join a dozen other fighters corralling the merc ships. A tug transits into space between Krmot's floating derelicts and our ship. It begins to grab the ships with tow beams and move back in system towards Sewer City.

"Where are they taking Krmot's fleet?" I say. "Why not just nuke these guys till they glow and shoot them in the dark?"

Kasha says, "I'm receiving a comm from Lieutenant Doar. It looks like the FTG has something special planed for them back at Sewer City. He can't say more."

"Un-Jun freighter, this is Oliver Med Vessel Twelve. Do you copy?"

A ship twice the size of our freighter has materialized in our front vid screen while we were yakking. Its hull is a brilliant white. Along the side are tall red letters spelling out 'FTG H.P. Oliver Med 12'. "Stand by for boarding on the starboard portal." The ship spins, moves closer to our hull. I hear the distinctive 'clank' as they anchor onto our ship.

Bolton keys the ship intercom and asks, "Mr. Arlo, is my father ready for transport?"

"I've got his med table standing by on the starboard portal. He's not doing well, Bolton, you need to get down here."

Bolton plays his hands across the console and says, "I've put the ship in standby mode. We're on our way."

He nods to Kasha and me and says, "I'll thank you later for the rescue. Right now Father needs us." He slides out the pilot's chair and slips past us at a run.

Kasha moves out of the tiny bridge and starts past me. "I don't know how you and your friend pulled this off, but you have my eternal gratitude." She reaches up and plants a tearful kiss on my cheek and then darts past me down the corridor.

OK. What? Me? Us? I am so confused.

"Jake!" yells Arlo over the ship intercom. "Get your pink ass down here, now, or we're leaving you behind!"

Chapter Twenty Five

Two of Doar's fighters escorted Med Vessel Twelve to the FTG 'H. P. Oliver', a Saber class battle ship. The big ship and its support fighters were still in the process of destroying an attempt by the GHA to aqua-form several of the worlds in this system.

Arlo and I are standing by the screens in the medical lab watching the chaotic ballet of battle surrounding the Oliver. There is a large debris field from the remains of at least three GHA aqua-forming ships drifting above the world the Oliver is orbiting. Little flashes of far off ship to ship battles flare in the black velvet of space around us.

Arlo taps the screen with the bandaged stump of his hand. "It looks like we arrived just in time to see the last of the GHA get their rubbery wet asses handed to them. I hope the Oliver was able to get here before another species was vaporized by those bastards."

I glance from the screen to G'radian's table. A doctor is twiddling dials and pushing buttons on the bed's console. Bolton and Kasha haven't left G'radian's side since we arrived. "Yeah. Me too, buddy. The Universe can be a damn ugly place."

My mind drifts back to that quiet little bungalow on the beach where Arlo and I used to just chill and soak up the sun. We were so totally ignorant, drifting from day to day in our own tiny little personal world. Souls were suffering across the galaxies and all I did was drink cold beer, ogle beach bunnies and complain about sun burn.

It feels really good to know that now Arlo and I are trying to protect and serve those worlds that cannot protect themselves. I have no idea if we're winning or losing, but I know it's worth trying.

The room portal cycles and two FTG officers enters the room. One motions for us to join Kasha and Bolton. We step up and trade salutes as best as our funky bodies allow. Navy training never sleeps.

The Captain shakes hands with Bolton and Kasha and nods to Arlo and me. "I'm Captain Spicer. I'm sorry I couldn't attend to you when you came aboard." He points to the vid screens and says, "As you can see we've been a little busy cleaning up the system."

He motions to the other officer and says, "This is Commander Sprague. He came to us from the Triumph just yesterday. Captain Starla asked me to personally check on two of her crew, Mr. Jasper and Mr. Arlo."

He looks at Arlo and me, obviously appraising us and says, "Your Captain gave me specific orders to verify your health, gentlemen." He points to the lack of an ear and my other scars and then Arlo's missing hand. "I see you've been knee deep in your own battles. Can I report that you are well enough to travel soon?"

Arlo says, "Yes sir. Just a few scratches. We would like to stay with G'radian until he recovers though."

Captain Spicer glances at the doctor and motions for her to move to the side of the room. "I need to talk to Lieutenant Sprinkle for a moment before we think about that, Mr. Arlo. Lieutenant." They move quickly and huddle up. I wonder what that's all about.

Command Sprague walks forward, shaking hands with Bolton and Kasha and nodding to Arlo and me. What are we, chopped liver? Oh. Yeah. Bloody claws and a mouth full of shark teeth. I get it now. Addressing me and my buddy he says, "You don't know how happy I am to see you alive, if a little worse for wear. Selenia has been chewing nails waiting to hear from you."

Arlo asks what I've been wondering this whole time. "About that, Commander. How the hell did you guys know where we were? Jake and I haven't had a chance to communicate with anyone for days."

Bolton steps forward and says, "I can answer that for you." He points to his father and says, "My father contacted me yesterday. He had overheard Krmot telling Crow that he had discovered your ruse. They were going to set up a fight and force you to fight to the death. He told me to contact the closest FTG outpost immediately and report that you had been exposed."

He pointed to the Commander and said, "I assume you were contacted by the FTG since I had to make the run back to Sewer City when Father called me again."

Command Sprague nodded and said, "Yes. Your message made it to the Triumph quickly. Captain Starla dispatched me with a squadron of fighters." Sprague turned to us and continued, "We've been hoping to hear from you for days. I've had this squadron on alert to scramble as soon we heard anything."

Well that clears that up anyway. "We're all grateful you were ready, Commander. To tell the truth I was pretty sure our gooses were cooked back in that fight ring."

Bolton nods to the Commander and says, "My father and I are obviously grateful as well, sir. Excuse me, I want to check on him." Bolton moves off the see to his father.

Kasha has been standing quietly, listening to the conversation. Her outfit is a mess, her face is still covered in blood and gore from the fight. I motion to her and say, "And there is someone else who will want to thank you." Kasha steps in front of the Commander and shakes his hand. "This is Kasha. She is one of the reasons Arlo and I are still alive."

Commander Sprague says, "A pleasure to meet you, Kasha." He smiles and then tilts his head to one side as recognition sets in. "Wait. Hmm. You bear a striking resemblance to …"?

Kasha drops his hand and smiles broadly. "Yes, Commander. I'm Captain Starla's sister. I've been a slave for almost eight years now. And for the record, if it weren't for these two I would still be a slave to that animal." She looks at the three of us and raises a finger. "I'll bring you all up to date later, I'd like to contact Selenia now if I can be excused."

"Of course!" Sprague exclaims. "There is a communication console just outside this room to your left that you can use. I'm sure Selenia will be thrilled to hear from you!"

"Thank you, sir." She turns to us and says, "Excuse me, my new friends." She gives each of us a quick kiss. "The first brew of your choice is on me as soon as things are settled." She rushes through the portal to make her call.

Sprague says, "Starla is going to burst at the seams when she hears you two rescued her sister! Selenia never gave up hope that Kasha was alive. She's been paying private investigators for years to find her, but to no avail. How did you …".

"Father!" Bolton's frantic voice stops Sprague in mid-sentence. We turn and rush to the table where the doctor is desperately manipulating the med console. The room portal cycles and a med team rushes in to surround G'radian. The rest of us move hastily out of the way, pulling Bolton with us.

A few moments pass and then the med team backs away and leaves the room. Lieutenant Sprinkle motions for us to move to the table where G'radian, eyes closed, is straining to take breaths.

Bolton moves up and takes his father's hand and glances at the Lieutenant expectantly. "What's going on? Can't you help him?" His voice is starting to rise in anguish. "Do something!"

The doctor puts a hand on Bolton's shoulder. "I'm afraid we've done everything we can for him, son. The damage to his spine and internal organs is beyond our ability to repair. I've just given him all the pain medication I can without killing him." He lowers his hand and says, "You need to say your good byes now." The doctor steps back.

"Bolton. Jake. Arlo." G'radian's voice is strained and faint. We all gather around the dying man.

His eyes flutter open and he points to Arlo and me. "Please forgive my son for his part in the ambushes." He sputters and winces as small flecks of blood spot his pillow. "It was the horror of losing my family that drove me to harass your supply lines." He eyes his son and continues weakly. "Bolton tried to bring me back from my torment, but I wouldn't be appeased." He coughs violently, more blood making small red spots on his white sheets.

His cough subsides and he seems to sink further into his pillow. "Revenge blinded me to everything else." He takes a shallow breath and says, "We never meant for anyone to die, I swear to you on my wife's grave. Only to harass and if possible find the bridge officers on the ship that destroyed my family."

He winces again, his voice this time barely audible. "I never killed anyone. I sold them to the slaver's guild as part of my revenge." He coughs again and turns his face to Bolton. "I kept a record of who we sold them to, son. It's in my locker. Get it. Find them. Help set them free. Use whatever money we have." He closes his eyes, his breathing becoming erratic.

The doctor steps up to the console, manipulating several controls. He turns to Bolton. "His body is shutting down, son. He only has a few moments."

Bolton squeezes his father's hand, tears starting to flow freely. I have no idea what to say or do. My heart is breaking, the scene bringing back memories of my wife's dying minutes so long ago.

G'radian opens his eyes slowly and says to Bolton, "I'm sorry, son. Promise me you'll help them. Promise me." His breathing starts to slow. "Promise me."

Bolton leans down and kisses his father's forehead. "I promise, Father."

G'radian's body seems to deflate into the bed but a small smile rises on his face. And then he's gone. The console erupts into alarms. The doctor reaches over and silences them and then moves back again. He puts his hand on Bolton's shoulder again and says, "We'll leave you with him, son. Take your time."

Lieutenant Sprinkle motions for us to step outside the room, letting the portal cycle close when we're all assembled in the hall.

Captain Sprague says, "The Oliver will be on station until this system is completely cleared and a support fleet can relieve her. I've contacted Triumph and received orders to bring you all home ASAP."

Across the corridor a portal cycles and Kasha steps through with a dazzling ear to ear smile. "I've talked to Selenia!" She looks at Arlo and me, struggling to keep her voice steady. "We have so much to thank you for! For rescuing me. For fighting for me."

I can see tears welling up her eyes. There is nothing so touching as a woman who is weeping with joy. I carefully put my paw on her shoulder and say. "Remember, Kasha, you fought for us too. Without your help we would all be dead or trying to breathe in space now."

Arlo brings out his Duke drawl and says, "That's right, little lady. Jake and I owe you a big pile of thanks." He nods to me and continues, "So Jake will be buying the first round back on Triumph. Right, buddy?"

He beat me to it again! I shake my head and say, "That's right. And the second, third, fourth and fifth if everyone can keep up." I lower my hand from her shoulder and try to show a serious pink bunny face. "We're all sorry that you had to go through all that, Kasha. I was only playing at being a pet to Arlo but you really were a slave to that animal, Crow."

Kasha stiffens, her eyes narrowing and her lips becoming a thin, hard line. "Thank you, Jake. We'll talk more about that when we get back to Triumph. I have some ideas I'd like to share with you, Captain Sprague and Selenia." She looks around at us and her smile fails.

"Oh no." She looks toward the med lab portal and murmurs, "Bolton's father. He didn't make it?"

Before I can answer, Bolton steps through the portal, his eyes red, his face sagging in grief.

He looks around at us and says, "I can't believe he's really gone." His shoulders start to tremble.

Kasha steps in before anyone can say anything. She pulls Bolton into her arms and holding him tight. "I'm so sorry. So sorry." She pulls back and Bolton stands straight. She says, "Your father saved my life. And the lives of these people as well. He was a hero."

Bolton brightens a little and says, "Thank you for that, ma'am." He looks to Captain Sprague and says, "I understand that you'll want to prosecute me for crimes against the FTG, sir. I only ask for time to take my father to our home world and send him to the next life as our beliefs require. Then I will accept any punishment you deem appropriate. If possible, I intend to fulfill my father's last wishes, to find and return those officers we sold into slavery."

Captain Sprague shakes his head and says, "I can't promise you anything, son, not until I've contacted FTG Headquarters and received instructions." He looks at Kasha and to Arlo and me and continues, "But I believe you've got a few friends here that will help you with your case." He raises an eyebrow at us.

Arlo pipes in, "Absolutely, sir. When you contact HQ, sir, you can tell them that Jake and I would be glad to accompany Bolton to his home world and see that he returns."

I shake my head in agreement. "Of course."

Chapter Twenty Six

FTG Headquarters agreed to allow Bolton two days to bury his father and return to the Oliver as long as Arlo and I agreed to be responsible for him. We agreed, of course.

Bolton put his father to rest in a family crypt in accordance with Un-Jun beliefs. The ceremony was simple and attended by hundreds of clan members. They all wore simple white robes and a small round blue cap that had silver writing all over it. G'radian was resting on a stone table in front of the crypt, his face was serene, smiling. He was also garbed in white, but his cap was dark red with tiny golden script all around it.

I was struck by the absence of open grieving and mourning. Instead of a dark, somber mood it was light and almost joyful. Everyone sang. Dozens of intertwining melodies, sung as one, seemed to flow like warm honey around the circle. Their voices lifted my spirit to the clouds. They joined hands and circled G'radian's altar, slowly moving around him, chanting and singing in unison.

One young woman had motioned for Arlo and me to join the circle saying, "He wants you to celebrate his life with us. Come join our circle."

Arlo and I did our best to move with the others. I didn't attempt to sing with my monster mouth but Arlo did a wonderful joyous of rendition of 'Amazing Grace' in his best Sean Connery voice.

When the ceremony was complete, Bolton and others moved G'radian into the crypt and closed it again. The crowd moved to an open area next to the crypt that had several large tents erected, food arranged on long tables. Everyone grabbed plates of food and stood in small groups talking about G'radian, Bolton and their family.

Arlo and I stood to one side watching this amazing display of joy and peace and wondering how these people must view life and death to be so happy at a funeral. The woman who had asked us to enter the circle came away from a small group and brought us each a small plate.

Her smile was infectious. "My name is Marlaa. I am one of Bolton's cousins. You are Arlo and Jake, the one's my Uncle saved, are you not?" She was dazzling in her white robe and soft light brown skin. Small silver and gold rings adorned her ears, nose and around the bone ridges of her tattooed cheeks. The white bone, tattoos and metal rings seemed to melt together like a marvelous surrealistic painting by Dali.

Arlo said, "Yes. Thank you for including us, Marlaa." He looked around at the crowd and said, "If you don't mind my saying, Marlaa, this seems more like a party than a funeral. Jake and I weren't expecting this."

Marlaa laughed and said, "Yes, I'm sure it must seem odd to you. I have studied other cultures and I must say I find the way others send their loved ones to the next life to be equally strange."

She turns and waves to encompass the scene around us. "To the Un-Jun, death is celebrated the same as life. We celebrate the passing of our souls to the next adventure because we are sure that it will be wondrous and full of new joys. We do not waste our 'yan-nay', what I believe you call your karma, railing against the ways of life, rather we embrace it. No one wants to die, but all do. Celebrate all you can in this world, my friends. Grieve some, celebrate much."

Bolton approached as we were talking. Marlaa said, "I will leave you now. It was an honor to meet and talk with you. Be at peace." She nodded to both of us, turned and waved to Bolton as they passed each other.

Bolton waved back to his cousin. "Marlaa is an amazing woman, is she not? Her husband is a lucky man. They have been a great comfort to me."

"Yes, she seems wonderful. She was explaining the celebration for your father's life," I said. "I find your culture's view of death to be compelling and beautiful."

Bolton nodded and said, "Thank you." He looks at each of us and says, "The ceremony is complete now. If you will allow me to share a while with my friends and family then we can leave."

I said, "Of course. When you are ready just let us know."

"Thank you. It will be very soon. All of our goodbyes were said yesterday while father's place was being prepared. I will return shortly."

The crowd had thinned quickly after that and Bolton was back in less than an hour.

He seemed at peace when he approached us, as though a weight had been lifted.

"We can go now. Thank you for coming and for joining our circle. It means a lot to me and father would be very pleased."

The trip back to the Oliver was swift and silent.

Chapter Twenty Seven

We dock in one of the H.P. Oliver's shuttle bays and walk down the ramp. At the bottom is Captain Sprague and an escort of four Marines. We stand at the bottom of the ramp and the escort forms a tight square around Bolton.

Sprague says, "This is a formality, Mr. G'radian, considering you and your father's crimes against the FTG and its colonies. Though I don't think it's needed, it is required by military protocols. Please follow me. Kasha, Mr. Arlo, Mr. Jake, I need you to come along as well." He turns and starts forward, our entourage in tow. We step up on a red transport tile and speed off into the bowels of the huge ship.

As we are zipping along Captain Sprague addresses us without turning around. His voice is amplified and the surrounding noise muted by the force field holding us to the tile. "The Triumph is currently engaged with other FTG ships in another quadrant. We will not be able to join her until the conflict is resolved. Captain Starla assured me this would be within a day or two at most. So we are going to convene a trial for Mr. G'radian here. We'll be linked to the FTG legal court via a virtual link. Unless you wish object to a speedy trial, Mr. G'radian."

Bolton says, "No, sir. I don't believe justice would be served by delaying this. I know my father would have agreed."

We enter the central shaft of the ship and turn 'up' towards the bridge end. The tile twists and zips us past the hundreds of other tiles, robots and assorted travelers, each under control of the ship's AI. Again I'm as always amazed that no one ever collides on these flying Frisbees. The central shaft reminds me of a bee hive filmed in ultra-high speed.

We zoom into deck level two, just below the bridge level, down a short corridor and settle near the outer hull. All but the Marines step off the tile.

Sprague salutes the Marines and turns to a portal outline. The tile zoom off with all four Marines still on board.

We enter the room and the portal cycles closed behind us. It's a small room, maybe twenty by twenty, with a small dais and podium on the right. A floor to ceiling vid screen displays the black vastness of space outside the ship.

Captain Sprague takes a position behind the podium facing us. He motions for Bolton to stand in front of the podium. "Kasha, Mr. Arlo, Mr. Jake, please stand behind the accused. I'm assuming you wish to speak for him during this proceeding?"

We agreed on the shuttle ride that if there was a trial here that Kasha could be our spokesman unless called on individually.

She nods and says, "Yes, sir. I will speak for all of us on his behalf."

"Very well. Ship, please connect us with Fleet Legal Courts. I notified them earlier to be prepared."

The Ship responds through the room intercom. "Yes, sir. The tribunal is standing by. Be aware that these proceedings are being broadcast throughout the galaxies." A hologram of three beings, standing behind a simple black and gold bench appears to Sprague's left. I recognize a Sensanite, a Grockna and a human. Each wears an FTG military uniform appropriate for their species.

On the right of the podium another hologram materializes. Standing in leg and wrist shackles are the captains of Krmot's pirate fleet, with Krmot front and center looking like a trapped rat. To one side there is another hologram of a lone human in FTG uniform, also in shackles.

Sprague points to the female human and whispers to us, "That is the spy at Fleet Headquarters that was feeding the mercenaries intel on supply convoys. We learned enough from interrogating the mercenaries to uncover her identity. Just in time too, she was preparing to escape on a freighter out of the Galaxy. She's going to be tried as one of the pirates."

Arlo nods. "Damn straight she should be, sir. There is a special Hell reserved for souls like hers."

The Grockna picks up a small golden hammer and strikes it three times against a golden bell on the bench, each strike ringing for several seconds. "This tribunal is called to order. The local authorities have agreed to let this court judge the defendants in all matters brought against them. Our decisions will be final and binding." All three judges sit at the same time.

"We have reviewed the evidence presented by the Federation and by the mercenary group based on Sewer City in the multiple cases of sabotage, savagery, theft, abduction and murder by the defendants. Is there anything the defendants wish to say before we pass judgement?"

The pirate ranks burst into jeers and raucous laughter, all except Krmot who seems to be melting into his boots. Hands, tentacles and other appendages form species specific versions of the universal 'up yours' symbols. Do these guys not understand what's happening? Lawlessness breeds contempt, I suppose. Personally I'd be shaking in my baggy pirate boots, just like Krmot. Not that I care about the bastard or any of his mates after all they have done.

Captain Sprague comes to attention and says, "I wish to make a motion that Bolton G'radian be tried separately due to the special circumstances I submitted prior to convening this tribunal."

"We have reviewed this information as well, Captain Sprague." The Grockna turns to each of the other two judges, each nodding approval. "We concur with the request, provided all the provisions of the resolution are implemented. If not, Mr. G'radian will return to this tribunal and receive the same sentence as the other defendants."

"We understand, your honors."

I ping Arlo, "OK, buddy. Do you know what Captain Sprague is talking about?"

He pings me back, "Not a clue, Jake."

Arlo starts to speak, "Captain Sprague, what request…"

A stern look for Sprague stops Arlo in midsentence. "Quiet."

All three judges rise. The Chief Justice says, "It is our verdict that the defendants are guilty of all charges."

I expected Krmot's mob to explode into riot. Instead a deathly silence prevails. I think reality just set in.

"The extreme crimes committed by the defendants demand an extreme punishment. Though the Federation condemns slavery in any form, we cannot rule on this complaint in as much as the local laws allow such a heinous practice. We can only hope that after viewing these proceedings the local governments will reconsider allowing this practice."

He turns towards the images of the mercs and continues, "On all other counts the maximum sentence has been set. All individuals will be relegated to the isolation penal planet 'Barre T'Ubat' for the remainder of their lives. There, each of you will be confined to a ten kilometer plot of land with no possible contact with any other sentient being. You will live and die alone. Sentence is to begin immediately."

Krmot's mob seems to deflate even further, most of them dropping their heads. Krmot starts to tremble and falls to his knees, his high squeaky voice crying out. "No! No! Please have mercy!"

The Chief Justice shakes his head and frowns, "You showed no mercy to the hundreds of beings you sold into slavery or murdered. This court will set an example for others in this quadrant that choose to commit crimes against all species, against the Federation and its allies." He faces forward, towards the billions of beings watching this broadcast. "You have been warned."

He rings the bell three more times and says, "This part of the trial is now complete." He nods to someone on his right and the image of Krmot, his gangsters and the spy fades. He strikes the bell one more time and says, "We are in recess for fifteen minutes." The hologram of the judges fades too.

Sprague turns to us and says, "All right. We have a few minutes for questions before Bolton faces his own trial."

He raises his hand to Arlo and says, "To answer your first question, I presented the request the judge mentioned. I asked that Bolton's circumstances be viewed in context with his father's obsession for revenge and his own loss of family due to an FTG error. I also brought out that none of the ambushes under G'radian had resulted in loss of life."

I speak up, "Why didn't you tell us about this?"

Sprague says, "You didn't need to know and I needed to be able to use your testimony if the court decides to question you. At any rate now you know."

Bolton says, "I appreciate your efforts, sir. But I don't understand why you would want to help me. What my father and I did, sending those people into slavery, was deplorable. I never understood why my father thought it could be justified."

Kasha places her hand on Bolton's arm and says, "You're right, it was deplorable. I can tell you from personal experience how horrible it is. Though most beings sold into slavery are not kept as combat pets like I was."

Captain Sprague continues, "The resolution the judge mentioned is the most important thing you have to consider, Bolton."

"What resolution, sir?"

"I've been in contact with Captain Starla on the Triumph and we believe that your father's last wish should be carried out as soon as possible. I volunteered to be the FTG's lead on finding and retrieving all the bridge officers your father sold into slavery. I have a vested interest in this quest since my convoy was ambushed and almost destroyed by the mercenaries under one of your father's Lieutenants, Rayt."

Bolton clinches at the name. "Rayt! I knew it! He tried to take over our operation because we refused to take civilian slaves. He didn't care about the convoy goods. He only wanted to destroy FTG ships and make money off the slaves he could capture." Running his hand through his hair he says, "He stabbed me in the back and my father killed him. Our ship's med doc was able to mend me enough to function."

Bolton bows his head and continues, "I'm sorry for your losses, sir. You must believe me that we gave strict orders to disable only, not destroy."

"I believe you Bolton. More importantly I have corroborating evidence that backs that up. Without it I would not have been able to convince the court to try you separately."

Arlo says, "So the court is going to decide on what, sir? What is the resolution?"

Captain Sprague nods to Bolton and says, "This is the deal, Mr. G'radian. You will retrieve your father's book and assist me in finding and freeing all the officers you sold into slavery. I will assume command of the frigate 'Levelland'. Until all officers are freed or accounted for you will remain in my custody. After we finish this mission you will serve prison time, the penal facility and length of the sentence at the discretion of another FTG court hearing. In addition, you will receive full medical attention for your wounds which, I'm assured, will fully repair the damage."

Kasha raises her hand and says, "I'd like to join your crew, Captain. I have a personal interest in ending the slavery trade in this quadrant. Maybe with the help of the Levelland and the backing of the Federation we can convince these people that this is a barbaric practice that must stop. When do you intend to start your mission?"

Captain Sprague seems to consider something and then says, "I can see where you would be an asset, Kasha, with your firsthand knowledge of the slave trade. To your question, my ship is being crewed now but I don't expect her to be ready for two more weeks. I assume you want to reunite with your sister on the Triumph?"

Kasha's face brightens and she nods. "Yes, I would." She turns to Bolton and says. "This won't be easy. Bolton. Slavery has been losing favor as the quadrant matures but it is still deeply ingrained in the local cultures."

She turns to Sprague and says, "I think you will find that the best approach to changing the attitudes about slavery will require political and financial pressures. Slavery is mostly about wealth. Those in power must see the advantage of ending the practice by seeing the pain of keeping it while others reject it."

Captain Sprague chuckles and says, "We are of a like mind there, Kasha. And the history of hundreds of cultures backs up that tactic."

Sprague raises an eyebrow to Bolton and says, "Well, Mr. G'radian? Will you accept this sentence? It means you'll remain in my custody until I decide there is nothing more we can do to retrieve our missing officers. You'll have no official standing other than civilian consultant, but you will be subject to all our military rules and regulations. Navy life is not easy, son, but I suspect neither was your life as a trader."

Arlo and I have a quick mental exchange. I raise a hand to get Bolton's attention. "Bolton. Before you answer, Arlo and I would like to say that we'll be in your corner if you ever need help. You and your father made mistakes, but in the end you came back for us when you could have left us to Krmot and his thugs."

Arlo says, "Yes. And your father paid dearly for helping us. We'd like to pay that back if we can."

Bolton looks around at the small group and says, "I am honored that you would do so much to help me." He looks at Captain Sprague and says, "I accept your offer, sir. Thank you."

He shakes Sprague's hand and then nods to the rest of us. "Truly. Thank you."

Three bells chime and the court image reappears in front of us.

"This court is now in session…"

Chapter Twenty Eight

"Are you sure you want to go back to being a puny bag of bones, Jake?"

Arlo's gravelly voice is distorted by the mucky mucus of the rejuv tank. His scaly face looks totally gross through the curved tank wall. He's still in his bio-morphed body waiting for me to revert to my beautiful human form. We played rock-paper-scissors to see who went first. It looked a little weird considering our clawed paws. It took three tries before one of us changed from scissors to rock. Go figure.

"Yes. As much as I love being able to slice through metal bars I'm ready for the pink bunny jokes to stop." This is true. I hate those jokes.

Our trip back to Triumph was delayed a few days while she finished her skirmish with a GHA aquaforming fleet. More like a full blown mega battle as the FTG had four Nova class battleships engaged in the conflict. It had been a hard won battle, but the squids were finally pushed out of the sector and most of the aquaforming ships destroyed. The GHA will be smarting from the losses for a while. I hope.

When we arrived Pixie and Nanel were waiting for us. After a quick meet and greet with Kasha and Bolton, Kasha had taken off to reunite with Captain Starla. A Marine squad was waiting for Bolton. Pixie and Nanel whisked Arlo and me off on a tile to the same lab where we had first bio-morphed.

Since I won the game they put me in the tank and filled it with the same bio-muck that they used to change me into a gigantic pink bunny monster. Now it was time to see if this process was really reversible.

Nanel's dazzling white uniform drifts towards me, her face distorted but still gorgeous. Like a Dali painting of the Mona Lisa. Or something like that. Pixie is standing next to her, a look of concern on her pretty face.

Nanel says, "If you are ready, Mr. Jasper, I'd like to proceed."

"Yes, ma'am, I'm ready. Just one thing, though."

"Yes, Mr. Jasper?"

"Please don't let me wake up pink. It's unmanly."

Nanel laughter would charm a mountain troll. "Relax, Jake. All our models show you'll revert to virtually your original body. Standby. I'm administering a sedative. You'll be unconscious for about an hour."

Wait, did she say 'virtually'?

Pixie and Nanel start to slide backwards down a quickly narrowing tube of light, like looking through a telescope backwards. I hope that's normal…

******

"Wakee, wakee, Buckoo. Hey! Jake! Wake up, lazy bones. You've slept long enough."

Arlo's voice feels like ice daggers in my ears. "Yo, buddy, I hear you. I hear you. Give me a second, OK?"

I must have dropped to the deck because I'm on my back, my eyelids stuck shut. I reach up to clear my eyes before I remember that I've got claws. But, instead of gouging my eyeballs out there is the wonderfully soft texture of fingers! Yes!

Squinting against the brightness of the lab lights, I look up. Nope, not still in the tank. I can feel the soft caress of a med table beneath me and a light sheet covering my body. I slowly feel my body through the sheet, from hairy head to waist. Yes, yes, yes! I'm back!

Lieutenant Commander Nanel leans over my face smiling. "Let's get you standing up, crewman." She grabs my arm to help me stand. The sheet falls away as I rise. It's awfully chilly in here. I look down slowly at my slightly damp body. Ahh. I'm all there! And it feels good! I wiggle a little to see if my toes and everything respond. Ahh. I'm back! Thank you, thank you, thank you!

There's a couple of snickers behind me so I turn to see Pixie, Nanel, Arlo and a med tech all grinning at me. The med tech bursts out laughing, then covers her mouth and says, "So sorry. It's just so cute!"

Pixie giggles and says, "That's enough, Pruett. You're excused now. And not a word of this!"

The med tech takes another look at my butt and then exits the lab. What the hell?

"What's she talking about Asa? What's cute? My butt? It's a manly butt, not cute! Right? Oh crap! What happened?"

I glance at my reflection of the console behind me. Crap! My butt is bright pink, from the small of my back and half way down the back of my thighs!

"What the hell!" I glare at Nanel and say, "You said this would be reversible, Commander! That," I point to my neon pink derriere, "was NOT there before!"

Pixie pipes up, "Relax, Jake. We said we believed it would be totally reversible. We also told you there were risks. You accepted the risks, remember?"

Pixie reaches up and turns my head. She frowns a little and says, "How does your ear feel?"

"What about my ear?" I reach up. The top half of my ear is gone! What the ….?

Nanel says, "It looks like some traumas are not reversible." She reaches over and exams my ear, twisting and turning it like a piece of rubber. "I don't know if we'll be able to fix that, Mr. Jasper. I'll have a med team look at options for you."

Pixie smiles and says, "I don't know, Jake, I think I kind of like it! Gives you a rakish, pirate kind of look. It suits you." She gives me a small mirror to see it with.

Holding the mirror to the side, I examine what's left of my gorgeous ear! Must have been that last fight with Kasha. Great. My hot girlfriend likes my notched ear. I can't say fix it now, no way. If she likes it, it stays!

Pixie takes the mirror from me and holds out a crewman's uniform. "Here, put this on so we can finish our exam. We'll talk about your butt later." She winks at me and hands me some shoes.

I don the uniform and slip on the shoes, wondering if it's possible that this won't end up on the ship's internal media site.

Still fuming, I say, "Right. Right. I know what I said, Lieutenant. And I meant it. I guess if this is the worst of it I'm pretty lucky."

Nanel folds her arms across her front and says, "Damn straight you're lucky, crewman. Now lie back down so we can complete the examination." She grins at me, "Other than your new coloration and the ear, your physical condition is looking good. I just want to run a deep molecular scan and compare it to your initial exams."

I lay down on the table again and it comes to life, little lights and bleeps coming from the console.

"What about you Arlo?" I look over at my buddy standing there with his upper arms crossed, squatting on his four legs. "When do you get reverted?"

Arlo nods his head and says, "Well, about that. It seems that the models are predicting that there's a fifteen percent chance that I would lose some or all of my telepathy. One model show a thirty percent probability that I would not remain sentient at all."

"Oh, damn, buddy!" Jeez, what he must be feeling.

I turn to Nanel and say, "What happened, sir? Why is he different?"

Nanel shakes her head and says, "We're not sure, Jake. Our best guess is that the bio-morphic fluid we've been holding in storage mutated somehow. As we said originally, this is an experimental procedure."

Arlo says, "It's ok, Jake. I talked it over with the Commander while you were gold bricking. I kind of like this new body, if you want to know the truth. She thinks that we can regrow my hand or at least get me a prosthetic hand to replace it."

Arlo leans down a little and says over our mental link, "And I don't want to lose the ability to talk my best friend." His beady eyes rotate a couple of times. "Who would keep you in line and kick your butt at chess?"

I say out loud, "Are you sure, buddy? It's your decision of course. It's your life." I grin and say, "Just so you know, if you stay like that no more shoulder rides. Understood?"

Arlo hoots out loud, "Understood, Jake."

This is going to be so strange, but I kind of like the idea now that I mull it over. Arlo will still be Arlo, but with a powerful body and a voice. I guess we'll have to see if it's a choice he regrets.

Pixie looks down from the console and says, "OK, Jake. We'll puts your implants in after you've both had some down time. For now, your scans are almost identical to the initial parameters. The reversion worked wonderfully. Expect of course for a couple of cosmetic alteration." She grins, obviously enjoying my predicament.

"Right. Cosmetic alterations."

Nanel taps a comtat on her arm, grins and says, "I've contacted the Captain about our status. She's waiting for us in crew's lounge twelve, something about the first round being on her. Remember that the specifics of you mission are classified for now. Understood?"

Arlo and I nod in unison. "Yes sir."

I sit up just as a tile floats into the lab. We step on and we're off.

Chapter Twenty Nine

We zip through the central shaft of the Triumph like a demented bee in a tubular mega hive.

Arlo pings me, "Feels good to me home, doesn't it Jake. I gotta say I missed this big, shiny, flying doughnut stack."

I ping back, "Yeah. I know how you feel, little buddy." *Oops.* "I mean, buddy. I guess I can't say little anymore, can I."

Arlo rolls his eyes at me and says, "Sure you can. Just remember that now you could ride on my shoulder instead of me on yours!"

The tile takes a tummy twirling twist and zips down a corridor and then into an open portal to our favorite crew's lounge.

It's a setup. The lounge is packed with crewmen, all dressed as whatever passes for casual in their culture, which from the looks of some of them is nothing all. Yikes! So that's where a T'eeK'ee's tentacles are attached to their bodies! That's an image I'm never gonna get rid of.

Everyone has a mug of some obviously inebriating liquid raised in salute as we land by the far wall, next to the vid screens. We're surrounded by a floor to ceiling spectacle of the soul stopping velvet black of deep space. Against the mind-numbing blackness there are hundreds of maintenance droids, small craft and crewmen in those egg shaped suits floating by in some kind of silent choreographed ballet.

"Pinky! Pinky!" "Kong! Kong!" erupts from the crowd.

Well, so much for keeping it a secret.

We step off the tile in front of Captain Starla, Kasha and the XO, Lieutenant Commander Betzel. All three are dressed in casuals. Kasha and Starla are definitely twins, dressed in loose light blue blouses and dark blue, calf length pants. The only way to tell them apart is Selenia has dimly pulsing comtats covering her body and the Kasha's is covered with her battle scars. I can't decide which is hotter. Hmmm.

Arlo has to yell to Pixie to be heard over the chants and cheers, "I thought our mission was still classified? How do they know about 'Kong' and Jake's shiny pink butt?"

Pixie smiles and leans close enough for both of us to hear, "How you were disguised is still classified, guys, but between the communications with contacts in Sewer City, the mercenaries televised trial, the appearance of Kasha and the rescue mission that Captain Sprague lead, it was pretty obvious what happened." She turns to Arlo and says, "I'd say 'Kong' is going to stick for a while. How do you feel about 'Kong, the Devastator'?"

Arlo nods and says, "'Kong, the Devastator'. I kind of like it. What about you, Pinky?"

Before I can retort my dislike for my new moniker the crowd goes quiet. I look up at the dais where Captain Starla who has raised a mug of beer for quiet. That's cool, never seen her do that before.

"All right, everyone, let's settle down." She points to us and says, "Someone get those people a brew."

A robo-server zips up with drinks for us. I grab an ice cold mug of my favorite recreated beer, a Fat Tire Amber Ale, and the others grab their drinks.

Starla raises her mug and says, "Alright. I'll make this short and sweet. We're videoing this ship wide so everyone can participate. We're here to celebrate the return of crewman Jake Jasper and his partner Arlo the Devastator."

The room erupts into cheers, laughter and applause. "No! Not Arlo! Kong and Pinky!" "Pinky. Pinky" "Kong." "Kong."

The Captain bows slightly to the crowd and says, "My mistake, my mistake. The return of Pinky and Kong."

The room goes nuts again. I look at Arlo and shrug. He leans in close and says, "No sense fighting it, Jake. You know that, right?"

He's right, of course. You can pick your friends. You can pick your nose. But you can't pick your friend's nose and you can't keep sailors from giving you a nickname. "Right."

Starla calls for quiet again. She motions to the whole room. "Every crewman on this ship has performed well above the call of duty, time and time again. Each time we celebrate you individually we also celebrate the whole crew. Kong and Pinky here are no exception. They have returned from an extremely dangerous mission. One which they accepted immediately, with no objections. One that could easily have cost them their lives."

She points to a Grockna standing in the back of the room. "Just like our Mr. Zahcore, whom we celebrated yesterday. His bravery under fire in our last engagement saved hundreds of civilians."

Zahcore bows slightly to the Captain and to the crowd. It's not possible with his species, but I believe he's actually blushing! Must be the lights.

"Zahcore." "Zahcore." "Zahcore."

Arlo and I join the crowd, shouting and raising our mugs in salute and then downing a deep swig. Damn that tastes good!

The Captain raises her hand again and says, "Yes. Now we celebrate these two crewman. Kong the Devastator and Pinky. Their mission was exceedingly dangerous and frankly it had little chance to succeed. But succeed they did." She looks at Kasha and continues, "And in that mission they also rescued my sister, Kasha, whom I thought was lost to me years ago."

I can see the tears start to well up, emotions choking her despite her legendary self-control. She's obviously having trouble maintaining her composure.

Time to jump in and save her. I raise my mug and say, "To be fair, ma'am, Kasha also saved our hides on more than one occasion." I reach up to touch my scalloped ear and continue, "Though she does have a weird way of showing appreciation."

Kasha's face turns a bright crimson. She winks and says, "I'm sorry, Jake." She starts to move towards me and says, "Let me kiss it to make it better." The crowd let's out a collective 'ooohhh'.

Pixie is suddenly in front of me with her hand extended, stopping Kasha in her tracks. "No you don't. That ear belongs to my boyfriend. I'll be doing the only ear kissing here." She reaches up and plants a wet kiss on my ear. It sends shivers down my spine.

Kasha steps back smiling. "Of course, Asa. I'll leave his recovery in your hands."

Pixie smiles back and says, "Good."

There's another collective murmur from the crowd. "Oh yeah, oh yeah, oh yeah. Uh huh." All the guys and some of the women are winking and giving me the thumbs up. I'm going to be hearing about this forever!

Kasha looks at Arlo and me and says, "I can't thank you two enough for freeing me. I will always remember you and your bravery."

The XO looks at us and says, "All right, all right. Save the rest for the privacy of your rooms." She raises her glass and waves to the room. "Let's raise a glass in thanks for the safe return of our shipmates, Pinky and Kong!"

The crowd starts to chant. "Kong!" "Kong!" "Pinky!" "Pinky!"

Arlo pings me and says, "You know what you have to do, right 'Pinky'? Or do I have to pants you?"

Fine.

I step up on the dais, turn around and drop my pants to show off my new badge of honor.

"Pinky!"

The Pink End

Made in the USA
Columbia, SC
01 November 2018